THE SKY AT Night

USA TODAY BESTSELLING AUTHOR
SAMANTHA LOVELOCK

For the broken.
For the brave.
For the ones who survived.
And for the ones we lost.

AUTHOR'S NOTE

This is a story of redemption and of learning to love yourself. We all have our bag of hammers to carry, and some are so much heavier than others. For a list of potential significant triggers, please visit: https://saman thalovelock.com/triggerwarnings

Want to stay up to date with all the latest news and happenings? Sign up for my newsletter today!

*"Find a place inside where there's joy, and the joy will burn
out the pain."*

- Joseph Campbell

light

CHAPTER ONE

Ty

"Ty, open the fucking door." Kess's voice filters through the fog of misery and self-loathing. Heavy fists bang out a staccato beat against the hollow-sounding wooden barrier that's the only thing standing between me and harsh reality.

"Not interested, Kess. Go the fuck away." The pristine marble is cold against my back, and my thin black T-shirt offers no warmth in the sea of white. Sitting on the floor, arms slung across my raised knees, I take in the ridiculousness of the hotel bathroom that's bigger than the apartment we grew up in. The observation makes me laugh, a flat, mirthless sound that bounces back at me off my stark surroundings.

"McInnis! I swear to Christ, if you don't let me in, I'll kick the goddamn door down and piss on your shoes for spite."

Ryan Kessworth knows me better than anybody alive. We were best friends long before this crazy ride started, and that's why I'm sure the threats aren't idle ones. The force of a zillion-dollar black motorcycle boot thuds against the wooden plank that separates us and shakes the vast expanse of mirror covering one wall.

Hoisting myself to my feet, I stumble and sway across the room to flick the lock before sliding back down the wall until my ass hits the floor.

"Happy now?" I mutter, angry and nauseous as the door opens and my bandmate and best friend is framed in the opening.

"This is how it's gonna be?" He studies me with eyes so icy blue, they're almost white.

"So, what if it is, asshole?"

Kess sighs at my belligerent response. He recognizes this ride. Stepping into the pristine white palace of my pain, his booted foot kicks the door shut behind him, cutting off the drone of the party raging outside.

"Fucking hell, would you look at this place? Why does the label always set you up with the biggest suite? Maybe once, ask them to give it to your guitarist?"

Opening the glass door to the shower large enough to park a car in, he takes a seat on the veined marble bench inside. A perfectly rolled joint and an engraved silver Zippo appear in the palm of his hand. I can't help but shake my head at how predictable he is.

And he probably thinks the same damn thing about me.

Lighting up, his long fingers lift the other end to his lips to take a deep drag. He leans back and stretches his legs out toward the shower drain, his gaze knowing and his exhale raw.

"He's gone, Ty."

My silence stretches thin and taut.

"Nothing you could have done would've changed anything," he tries again.

"I know." And the thing is, I *do* know. It all comes flooding back, the blood rushing in my ears and heart pounding in my chest the sickening soundtrack to my memories.

Heroin Heartbreak had a break in our schedule last Christmas, so I decided to surprise my dad. From the second I walked through the door, he was different. Thinner. Quieter. Not that he'd ever been overly talk-ative, but something had changed. It was months before I found out just how bad things were.

We were mid-way through our second world tour when the desperate phone call came from Maggie, the woman Dad had been dating for the better part of a year. She begged me to talk some sense into the pig-headed man she'd grown rather fond of, and she told me everything.

What started as treatable prostate cancer had metastasized to his lungs.

He was hell-bent on ignoring the advice of all of his doctors.

And he was dying.

Kess persuaded the label to postpone a string of shows, either by force or charm. I didn't much care which because I was on a plane before they stop me. My dad and I had words—sharp, jagged ones that cut to the bone and laid the truth bare. Faced with my unapologetic fury at his behavior, he caved and agreed to start treatment.

Money has the obnoxious ability to galvanize people into action, even doctors. Within two days, Dad had his first round of chemotherapy. It seemed to go reasonably well, but the puking started a few hours after we got home and didn't stop until the following afternoon. Scared shitless and sick as hell, he was dehydrated and exhausted. It took Maggie and I both to force him to swallow a few mouthfuls of water before he finally, mercifully, fell asleep.

Dozing in the recliner I'd moved next to the bed, I was yanked back to full consciousness a few hours later. At first, I thought he was talking to me. It took a few beats to realize the intense conversation was actually with Parker Twilling, an old high school buddy of his.

Which would have been perfectly normal if said buddy hadn't been killed in a car wreck eight years earlier.

It was surreal. He was insistent his bones were

burning from the inside, and his brain was cooking in his skull. That we were all trying to murder him, kept stealing his wallet, and that his socks were too tight. Full of gibberish and riddles, his thoughts made little sense as they left his dry, cracked lips.

But then he turned his attention to me and latched onto my wrist with incredible strength. Eyes locked on mine, he made a stunning confession. One he would never have let slip if he'd been in his right mind.

He admitted he had refused treatment when the cancer was first diagnosed because he was afraid of being perceived as anything less than a virile, solid, ladies' man. He worried he wouldn't be able to get it up anymore. Wouldn't be able to please the women he'd adored since he hit puberty and ogled his first titty mag. Wouldn't be able to fuck. And that would make him less of a man in his eyes, so he pretended it wasn't real.

He slept for thirteen hours straight after that. Woke up himself again, sane and stoic, and neither of us ever mentioned that night. Even if he did remember what he said, did it matter? Lambasting him for being a macho idiot wasn't going to change anything. His pride had already been pillaged by the disease—I wasn't about to snatch what was left.

Just shy of a week later, right before his second treatment, he all but forced me back on tour, dismissing my arguments before I voiced them.

"You made a commitment, and you'll follow it through.

It's the North American leg of the tour, so you'll be on the same damn continent. You can come home and visit whenever you have a break in your schedule. You will not sit here, wailing and wringing your hands like an old woman."

It almost killed me to leave, but he was unyielding. Dad watched how hard Kess and I worked to make it, and he was proud of us. There was no way he was going to let us jeopardize it all. The doctors had given him sixteen to twenty-four months, and once the tour was over in six, I planned to come back and stay with him. Until then, I allayed a modicum of my guilt by flying home, even just for a day, whenever possible. And each time, he was still my dad.

Until the last time.

When I flew home a week ago, the combination of the disease and its treatment had ravaged his body. It had choked him, stealing his breath and the fire in his eyes. My six-foot-three, broad-shouldered, burly father had been reduced to a gnarled shell, hunched and painfully thin, with eerily pale skin and patchy hair. Again, I tried to stay, but we were at the end of the tour. He argued up and down that he'd made it this far; another week wouldn't make a difference. Maggie backed him this time and was adamant I left.

Reluctantly, stupidly, I agreed to finish out the last handful of dates, and then I'd be back.

I should have recognized his plan all along. That

somehow, through all the pain and fear, his last thoughts would be to protect me.

"Two days." The words are strangled by the grief flooding my mouth. "The tour is over in two days, then I would have been home and been with him at the end." My blood burns with whiskey and regret.

"Brother," Kess's voice is laden with his own grief, "I've been in awe of your old man since he took pity on the seven-year-old runt who lived next door. He cared enough about a relative stranger to give me a safe place away from the swinging fists of my mother's dirtbag du jour." He pauses to clear the emotion from his throat. "So, I'm comfortable saying this with all certainty. There is no way he would have let you watch him die. He was too proud and loved you too much to have that be the last image of him you carry around in your head."

My rational mind understands what he's saying is true. But the knowledge does little to ease the awful ache in my chest or lessen the gnawing in the pit of my gut.

"I was a shitty son, Kess." My words are muffled by the palms of my hands now covering my face.

The boy who started as the new kid next door and quickly became family almost chokes to death on his last pull from the joint. Coughing, he stubs out the cherry against the sole of his boot before standing and waving the smoke away from his face.

"Ty, nobody in their right mind would ever label you

as a shitty son. Remember the first paying gig we ever played? That hellhole dive downtown? I spent my cut on beer and burgers with Sherry Lalonde in an attempt to get laid. You went home and paid the electricity bill. Shit, you bought your dad a *house* the first chance you had."

I heave myself off the cold marble tile and move to the mirror where Kess now stands, scrutinizing the hint of blonde scruff edging his jaw in his own attempt at keeping it together.

Dark and light, the two of us, brothers by choice rather than blood. Our differences have always been an integral part of our bond, as much as the things we have in common.

Unhappy with the gravitational pull of being upright, my head starts to swim. I lean forward to press my forehead to its reflection, and squeeze my eyes shut, waiting for the room to stop moving.

Maggie was the one who called to deliver the news this morning, and the first thing I did was stumble my way to the hotel bar. Five double vodka and sodas later, I threw the bartender four crisp hundred-dollar bills and returned to my room, a bottle of Balvenie single malt in hand. Smooth as hell going down, but I know from experience that's not the case when it comes back up. And it *is* going to come back up.

The nausea crests, bringing my old friend self-loathing along with it. I never wanted to be here again, teetering on the edge of destroying everything I've worked for.

Kess's usually pleasant baritone sounds like a million pissed-off little bees, and I sense I'm in real trouble. His big hand claps me on the shoulder as my vision pinwheels, and the whole place goes ass-over-teakettle.

the bright
lightly swings

CHAPTER TWO

Ty

The bass drum thumping away in my skull drags me out of nightmare landscapes. It takes a minute, but I manage to crack my eyelids open and squint at my surroundings. The attempts at homey touches do little to mask the impersonal sterility of the high-end hotel room.

I run my hand over the space beside me.

Alone. Thank fuck.

"Housekeeping." The tittering falsetto opens both eyes a little wider, and a grin pushes through the hang-over fog.

Wait, is it a hangover if you're still drunk?

"You better have coffee, asshole." My voice shreds more than usual this morning, the sandpaper sound mimicking the surface of my eyeballs. The dryness of my

throat brings on a cough that turns the bass drum into a full-fledged cranial marching band.

Kess walks into the suite's primary bedroom and dangles two white to-go cups over my head, the familiar green mermaid logo on each taunting me. I reach to snatch one greedily from his fingers, but he turns with a rude chuckle to set it on the nightstand instead.

"I'm hoping last night wasn't a prelude to what's coming down the road. You were throwing some serious red flags, and neither of us wants a repeat performance. I'm worried about a relapse, brother, so I have to ask, are we doing this shit again?" His tone is neutral as he drops into one of the white leather chairs in the bedroom's sitting area. I hold still for a five-count, then push myself to a sitting position.

"Doing what again?" I play dumb.

He raises a brow but doesn't say a word, unfazed by my bullshit.

"Oh, you mean the thing where I attempt to drown myself in booze and pussy until I manage to burn out all the pain or die trying?" The words come out more far more harsh sounding than intended, powered by guilt, anger, and shame.

He doesn't flinch and doesn't respond.

I stand and stride to the nightstand. Grabbing my coffee, I down a third of the almost-too-hot dark roast and enjoy the punishing burn the liquid leaves behind.

"No, we're not doing that again. I like to think I've grown up a little since then."

Kess pointedly eyes the rumpled sheets on the bed, then the empty bottle of scotch on the floor.

"What? So, I had a few drinks. After the news I got yesterday, I think I was entitled." I drop my coffee cup back on the nightstand and go in search of clean clothes. "Besides," I yell from the walk-in closet's depths, "it can't have been that wild of a night; I was alone when you barged in here."

"You weren't the first time I showed up."

His words hit like a punch to the solar plexus.

Damn it. Damnitdamnitdamnit.

Armed with a pair of dark jeans and a vintage Black Sabbath T-shirt, I throw them at my best friend's head and slam the closet doors in frustration.

"Way to bury the lead." The sheets hold a faint floral perfume and the musk of sex when I throw myself back onto the bed. My pounding headache must have taken priority when I woke up, and I missed the telltale signs.

"Where'd she go?"

"Off to tell her friends she fucked a real live rock star, presumably." He shrugs.

"You're a dick, you know that?"

He nods in agreement.

We sit in silence for a minute or two before he speaks gruffly from his chair.

"I can disappear with you this time if you want company." His offer is genuine, and I'd love to take him up on it, but this bag of hammers isn't his to carry. Besides the fact that he's not the one with the looming potential relapse, he's the only one I trust to have my best interests in mind during my absence. That loyalty is, in a way, one more thing I can thank my dad for.

The first night I met Kess, I stood warily in the doorway while he sat at our scratched kitchen table and scarfed Spaghetti-Os like they were his last meal. Scrawny, awkward, and skittish, he was unlike any other seven-year-old I'd ever met.

After the initial invitation, he would show up around dinnertime every few days, eat like he was starving, help with the dishes, then leave. He didn't say much more than 'please' or 'thank you' at first.

Those dinner drop-ins went on for about a month. Then something woke me up one night. The luminous hands of the little clock on my nightstand told me the sun wouldn't rise for hours yet. The floorboards were cold against my bare feet as I crept down the hall, the Spiderman flashlight I clutched my only weapon against the dark.

A woman's scream sliced through the silence, followed by the sound of something slamming into the other side of the living room wall multiple times.

Everything after that happened in flashes.

Dad picked me up and planted me firmly on the couch with orders not to move, while Kess's usually small voice bellowed in pain from next door.

Gripping my flashlight between my knees to free up my fingers, jamming one in each ear while I squinched my eyes shut tight.

The sudden sinking of the couch cushion next to mine, my eyelids flying open to find Kess beside me, terror etched on his features, a smear of blood across his lip.

Handing him my most prized possession, that Spiderman flashlight, because instinctively, I knew he needed it more than I did right then.

His small knuckles fish-belly white as he gripped it tight.

That night, Dad beat the shit out of Ms. Kessworth's boyfriend, and forcibly removed him from the four-story walk-up we lived in. Afterward, he found the two of us sitting stock-still on the couch, frozen in our shared fear. He washed Kess's face, told him he was proud of him for trying to stick up for his mom, and grabbed an old pillow and blanket from the closet.

From then on, more nights than not found the neighbor's kid sleeping on my bedroom floor. We became best friends, and it was a rare occasion you saw one of us without the other somewhere close by. After about six months, we came home from school and found my rickety single bed had been replaced by somewhat less rickety bunk beds. Ms. Kessworth had nothing to say—she didn't care where her kid slept, as long as it didn't interrupt the parade of losers she chose to share her own bed with.

My dad saved Kess, and Kess saved me. Without Dad's intervention, who knows how either of us would have turned out?

When the well-aimed empty to-go cup bounces off my temple, I realize I've been stretched out on the rumpled hotel bed lost in the past.

"Earth to space cadet." The words are laced with wry humor, but my best friend's face is pure concern.

"Sorry. Fuck, I think I'm still wasted." I scrub a hand across my face on my way to the bathroom.

"Which brings up my earlier question—are we doing this again?"

I turn the water on full and hot, drowning out anything else he might have said. Stripping off my boxers, I duck under the spray, and it takes all of a minute to realize my mistake. The water temperature, the alcohol still in my system, and the undeniable awful truth that my dad is gone are a terrible mix. Flinging open the glass door, I leap from the shower, naked and dripping, barely making the toilet before the contents of my stomach erupt.

Why did I listen to him? I'm such a fucking idiot. I never should have left. Screw the tour, the band, everything. He died alone, and I'll never forgive myself.

My eyes tear up from the force of puking, or at least that's what I try to tell myself.

I finish my shower, wrap one towel around my hips, and walk back into the bedroom, using another to dry my hair. Kess is still in the same chair, only now he's got my white Gretsch Falcon acoustic with him, long fingers picking out a mournful tune.

"You okay, Brother?" The question is casual and asked without eye contact, but the weight and worry behind the words are heavy. He continues to pluck the strings of my favorite guitar.

"Not in the slightest, and I won't survive a repeat of what happened that summer. So, tell Steady and the boys I'm going home to bury my dad. Refund the last two shows, play them with another singer, put Steady on stage Riverdancing, I don't give a fuck. I'm out."

"And?" This time his eyes meet mine.

"And as soon as everything is taken care of, I'll go back to The Overlook."

"He was a dad to me, too. You're out, I'm out. We'll go back together, and you can leave to pull your head out of your ass after the funeral. I'll meet up with Steady and the boys and keep things running on this side." Standing, guitar neck in one hand, he reaches for the phone in his pocket with the other. He pauses, looking at me for final confirmation.

"Make the call."

The jet was available to me as usual, but I turned it down. Normalcy was something I craved these days, an itch that begged to be scratched, and private planes don't scream normal. That meant flying commercial from New Hampshire to the west coast. I hadn't done it in a while, and Kess tried to warn me after the funeral, but I refused to believe the simple act of catching a flight would be a problem.

"O-m-geeeeeeeee." The squeal makes my right eye twitch and my teeth grind. "You're Ty McInnis." A scraggly, skinny blonde walking toward me from the arrivals area stops cold. Filler-heavy lips curl back in a predatory smile, and the tiny gem stuck to one of her eye teeth glints in the stark overhead lights.

Oh shit.

Before I can turn and duck into the men's room, she's on me like a spider monkey. She may think she's hot shit, but all I want to do is extricate myself from the steel grip of this stage five clinger with stale cigarette breath. The curious stares of nearby onlookers bore into my skull, and it's only a matter of time before they figure out why this girl is all but humping my leg.

The blonde loosens her hold to scramble for a selfie. I use the opportunity to push her away—hard enough that she gets the picture, but not so hard that she falls on her ass. Yanking the hood of my black sweatshirt up with one hand and grabbing my duffel with the other, I take advantage of a large, loud group passing by. Using their boisterous behavior as a barrier, I put their noise and flamboyance between myself and the superfan and don't stop until I'm through security.

Once I'm tucked into a darkened booth inside the closest restaurant, I risk exposing my face and order a drink from the wide-eyed waitress. Swallowing half of it, I pull out my phone.

> Dude, smack me in the head the next time I ignore you.

I will gladly smack you any time, Brother. What happened?

> Groped by an unknown female three feet in the door.

Was she cute?

> Not unless you go for the rabid groupie look.

There's something to be said for rabid groupies. Especially if they have big tits. Did she have big tits?

> Stop thinking with your dick, dick.

Yeah, like that'll happen.

The easy, familiar banter eases some of the tension tightening my temples and etching my jawline. Half-melted ice clinks against my teeth with the last gulp of my vodka and soda, as the announcement comes over the terminal loudspeakers.

"United Flight 4465 with service to Seattle now boarding."

Pulling my hood back up, I fire off a last quick text to Kess and jam my phone into the back pocket of my jeans. I'm out the door with a twenty on the table and a wink in the waitress' direction.

The line at the gate isn't too bad and only five people stand between me and the counter. Make that six. A kid peeks out from around a woman in pants tight enough to make my nutsack cringe in empathy. He looks about ten or eleven and visibly bored out of his tree. The woman, who I assume is his mother, chats up the man in the ill-fitting suit ahead of her, ignoring her son. His gaze darts around the room, his reaction priceless when it lands on me. He doesn't say a word, just stares at me, eyes round and mouth open. I glance down at his T-shirt and Heroin Heartbreak's latest album cover is emblazoned across the front.

"Nice shirt." I give him a grin and an appreciative nod. His answering smile is snaggletoothed but huge and lights up his too-thin face.

"Thanks, man," he lisps quietly. Not quietly enough, though. Tight Pants grabs him by the arm and starts giving him shit for talking to strangers. When she swings around to turn her wrath on me, it takes precisely seven seconds for her brain to catch up with her running mouth.

"Listen here, asshole, don't try to be all pervy with my kid. You leave him th—holy shit, you're the lead singer of that Heroin band, aren't you?" And in the blink of an eye, Suit Guy is forgotten. Smoothing down her second-skin V-neck shirt, she strikes the perfect pose to ensure an eyeful of her jutting tits and that vicious camel toe. "I had no idea you'd be even better looking in person."

Her kid looks mortified, watching his mother shamelessly hit on me. With a shudder, I avoid making eye contact and shove my way to the front of the line, fist-bumping the kid on the way. Sure, I come across as an entitled ass to everybody else waiting their turn but fuck it. I need to escape the cloying, sticky-sweet perfume of the woman I wouldn't touch with somebody else's dick.

"Mr. McInnis? Sir, the captain has announced our descent." The perky flight attendant's face comes into focus as the haze of sleep falls away from my eyes. "I need you to fasten your seat belt, please."

I murmur my acknowledgment and fumble for the buckle, satisfaction permeating my grogginess when the two ends meet and click. The telltale pressure builds in my ears the lower we get, and I force a few yawns to equalize it.

We must hit a rogue updraft because the plane suddenly judders for a few seconds, with a quick jolt up followed by a sharp one to the left. The same flight attendant gives me a reassuring smile from where she's strapped into the jump seat outside the cockpit door.

As we level out again, I drag my attention away from the small, white, nondescript smudge on the bright blue of her sleeve, and turn toward the window beside me. I catch a glimpse of Mt. Rainier before the sparkling water of the Sound itself comes into view. The knots of tension in my shoulders start to dissipate. When the wheels finally hit the runway, I realize how much I'm looking forward to this break.

By the time I've grabbed my duffel from the baggage carousel, I believe this break might be just what I needed. While it may not be a full-fledged smile, for the first time since my dad's funeral, the corners of my mouth are at least tilting in a positive direction, so that's something.

In a better mood than I have been in way too long, I decide to grab a coffee before I meet my driver. Oblivious to my surroundings, I stride straight to the barista and give her my order.

"Excuse you, asshole," a female voice snarls from behind me. "Wait your fucking turn."

"Good lord! Watch your language, please," the woman with her chastises.

"Watch it do what, exactly?" she bites back.

I turn to apologize for jumping the line and lose command of the English language when all the blood in my body rushes to my dick. I'm transfixed by impossibly blue eyes, curves for days, and full lips made for kissing.

Or biting.

Or sucking.

None of that is what grabs me by the balls, though. Instead, it's something in her stance and the innate, unspoken understanding that this girl would never back down from a dare. That she'd stare your bullshit straight in the face and call you on it.

Even better is the fact that there isn't a single lick of recognition on her beautiful face. Whether it's because my features are hidden by the hood covering my head or because she legit doesn't recognize me doesn't matter. Being nameless and faceless at this moment is a breath of fresh air.

Before I can squeeze a word out, she rolls her eyes and pushes past me to spit her order at the confused employee behind the counter. I join her at the pick-up area, still trying to figure out how to make my mouth work. My order is ready before her half-calf whatever non-fat double whatzit, and as I tilt the cup to my mouth, she fakes a stretch and jams her elbow sharply into my ribs.

As she grabs her drink from the barista, the light catches the ring she wears on her middle finger, the green stone seeming to wink at me. She turns, and with a nasty snicker at the hot coffee dripping down my chin, grinds her stiletto boot heel into the top of my foot. Ignoring her companion, she sashays out the door like she's walking a fucking Paris runway, leaving me stunned and fuming in her wake.

the right
lightly swa

CHAPTER THREE

Ty

As we make our way north on I-5, the driver is all business, maintaining a solid twenty over the speed limit and keeping small talk to a minimum. Once we board the ferry, I elect to stay in the car given the tender spot on my ribs, what's definitely going to be a bruise on my foot and the fact I'm wearing half my coffee.

I dig out my phone and flip through the digital photo collages Dad's girlfriend Maggie made for my last birthday. My teenage past grins up at me, one arm looped over Kess's shoulders, the other around my dad's. Seeing the three of us together, I can't help the smile that twitches my lips, even if it brings the ache of what I've lost with it.

From the beginning, Heroin Heartbreak was every-thing for Kess and me. Our music was an expression of who we were, therapy after all the shit we'd gone through, and a temporary escape from our blue-collar futures.

Kismet or fate or sheer dumb luck dropped us a gift right before our nineteenth birthdays. Nick Steadman—Steady to his friends—was in town visiting his sister who dragged him out for a beer. He spent our entire set that night eyeballing us over the rim of a perennially full pint glass.

The next day he became our manager.

In three months, we went from paying for our beer with scrounged change and playing fourth-hand instruments, to having a label, contracts, and an album. Life was suddenly exhilarating and intense and insane. Pussy followed us everywhere, often bearing booze and drugs. There were nights that seemed to last for days. Our first single went platinum, and Heroin Heartbreak became bonafide rock stars almost overnight.

I can't believe we almost lost it all because of one crazy, opportunistic bitch.

The driver returns to slip behind the wheel just before the slight swaying of the vehicle ceases. "We've docked, Mr. McInnis. I'll have you at your destination in no time."

The leather complains quietly when I shift in my seat and lean my head back, letting my mind wander through one of my biggest fuck ups. The one that prompted my introduction to The Overlook.

Kess found me passed out on the living room floor of the house he and I shared in the Hollywood Hills with an empty fifth of Johnnie Walker Blue clutched in my fist. Other than a vague recollection of being dragged by my heels through the main level, my memory of the last half of that night is still black as pitch.

I came to fully clothed, soaking wet, and freezing. Propped up under the icy cold spray in my onyx-tiled shower, I could blearily make out Kess's lips moving, but my alcohol-soaked brain refused to process anything he said. My entire body, fuck that, my entire world, had been ripped apart and jammed back together in the wrong order, minus a few pieces. Kess told me later that we stayed in the shower for a good thirty minutes before I started making any kind of sense, and he was confident I wasn't going to die of alcohol poisoning.

Steady made the call to his niece that night. I'll never forget puking my guts out on a private jet bound for Washington state, while my family's unfortunate history was being used as rating fodder by news media across the globe.

This trip back to Puget Sound is like coming home. Most people would look at me sideways if I said that out loud, given what The Overlook is. But it's where I picked up all my pieces, the ones the darkest parts of the music scene and my cunt of a mother tried so hard to steal. Now that I'm back, I hope it can work its magic again.

The gravel of the curving drive crunches underfoot

as I step from the back of the hired car and move toward the woman waiting for me.

"Ty." My name falls from her lips in equal parts welcome and disappointment.

Music lover, confidant, and all-around ass-kicker, Steady's favorite niece Mari is like a big sister to me.

Engulfing her in a brotherly bear hug, I can sense the conflicting emotions emanating from her.

"Mari." Exhaustion weighs heavy in my tone. "I've missed you."

"I've missed you, too, Ty." She steps back, squinting as she gives me a once-over. "I hoped I wouldn't see you back here under these circumstances again."

Offering everything from detox to rehab to straight-up mental health support, The Overlook has become one of the premier and most discreet wellness retreats in the United States. Favored by everybody from bad-boy rock stars to bratty TV tweens, privileged political night-mares to the spoiled kids of the obscenely wealthy, it has a waitlist a mile long. But Mari's got a huge heart and grateful clients with deep pockets. Donations and star-studded fundraisers make it possible for her to welcome people with limited means at no cost. She's always made it crystal clear it's not about the money for her; it's about helping the lost find themselves before it's too late.

"It's different this time. Preemptive." She's the only female in my life I've ever trusted or been able to be completely honest with. "You taught me to recognize the signs, and Kess made sure I did something about them."

"It's not your mom again, is it? She didn't—", her eyes widen.

I take a deep breath, emotion thick in my throat. "My dad died."

Her brows soften and her mouth forms a tiny 'o'. She hugs me again, a bone cracker this time.

"Ty, I'm so sorry. You two were so close." She steps back, sniffling. "When Kess called, he said you needed a spot. He didn't tell me what was going on, the stupid ass." Swiping a finger under each eye, her smile is small and sad. "Your cabin is ready. Why don't you go get settled? Same one as last time, as requested, and it's all yours."

I sling my bag over my shoulder, and we climb the wide porch steps.

"Thanks for making room for me, Mari. I know how long the list is."

"You're family—there's always a spot here for you. But it's my hope that you won't need it again."

The sound of a car engine in the distance signals another new arrival, and the vehicle turns off the highway to start down the long gravel driveway that winds through the trees.

"Go unpack and change." She wrinkles her nose. "Eau de spoiled milk and coffee dregs is unattractive."

"We both know I've smelled worse." I point out with a laugh.

She opens one of the massive front doors and playfully shoves me through it before turning to go back down the stairs to wait for the car moving at a snail's pace.

Not much has changed since the last time I was here. The lingering lavender and woodsmoke scents still tease my nostrils with the comforts of home. And though the face behind it is new, the same enormous cherrywood desk still sits along the back wall. I offer a small wave as I walk by, not wanting to be rude but having zero desire to engage in conversation.

Out back, the whole area is deserted except for two guys in sweats playing frisbee down on the beach. My lungs expand with what feels like my first true breath since the funeral, and my shoulders drop. If there's anywhere that can help me deal with the heaviness of my grief and overwhelming guilt, it has to be this place. I follow the familiar path to my cabin, happy that the door still has the same raspy hinge. My lips curve when I step inside, the rich and heady scent of cedar welcoming me, and I drop my bag with a sigh of relief.

CHAPTER FOUR

Hali

An elegant, black town car is waiting outside for us when we emerge from the airport. Surrounded by expensive leather and the faint whiff of fancy cigars, what was supposed to be an hour and forty-minute drive along the coast of Puget Sound has gone way past that. The driver appears to be allergic to the gas pedal and even got us lost once. But as much as I want to berate him for his unsuitable career choice, I bite my tongue. It's not really him I'm pissed at anyway.

The woman next to me gets that honor.

I'd jump in front of a train rather than admit it to her, but a secret, hidden, part of me is looking forward to being anonymous for a while. To leave her, my monsters, and the mess I made in Folkestone, behind.

The scene of all my dirty deeds lies on the edge of San Francisco Bay, north of the bright lights of the big city. Nestled in amongst thick trees that embrace the cliffs like long-lost lovers, are the homes of some of the most powerful families in the world. The same families whose entitled offspring have a few choice names for me.

Mean girl.

Bitch.

Cunt.

And they're right.

But they're wrong, too.

They've only ever seen what he allowed me to show them, what my father crafted and curated. Not a single person on this earth knows the real me, and that sure as hell includes the woman glaring at me with eyes strikingly similar to my own. "Can you please try to understand why this is necessary? That I'm only doing what's best?" My mother, Eleanor Torsten, now so dramatically different from the broken puppet of my childhood, grimaces.

"What's best for *you*, you mean?" I mock. "Because how the hell would you have any idea what's best for anybody else? That would require you to pay attention to somebody other than yourself, and we both know you haven't done that, well, ever." The idea is so absurd I have to bite back a laugh.

"How can you say such a thing? You're my daughter. Of course, I pay attention".

"Okay, I'll bite. What's my favorite color?" I watch in

sick amusement as her face goes from healthy tan to pale white to flustered tomato. She knows she can't answer the question, and worse, she knows I know. I snort in disgust and lean my head back against the seat.

Sure, part of me prays this little exile turns out to be the thing that sets me free from the rotting cage my father built. But the awful, petulant, bred-to-be-bad part of me still wants to throttle my mother with the pretty indigo Hermes scarf knotted around her throat.

For hinting at taking credit for any good that might come of this banishing.

For the horrific indecencies she let him commit and her milk-toast complacency for years and years.

For all the things she didn't do.

This is her fault as much as his.

"Hali, seriously. Does everything always have to be so dramatic with you? Can't you be good and do what you're told for once?"

"Oh, don't you worry, I've been doing what I'm told for a very long time, and I'm *exceptional* at so many things." The familiar sneer slips into place, curling my upper lip. "Not the least of which is telling it like it is, so let's be honest with each other here, Eleanor." Her jaw clenches at my use of her given name. "You're all better now, and it's so much easier to have your life back without dealing with me. Ding dong, the witch is gone. Everybody will be so happy for you. They'll probably have a fucking parade." No matter how hard I try to tamp it down, to keep my voice flat, an edge of miserable dismissal slices through the callous mean-girl mask I'm trying like hell to maintain.

"What else have you done? Why are you so certain they hate you so much?" A flicker of fear dances across her features before she squashes it. "It can't be that bad." Switching gears, she dismisses the unpleasantness with a wave of her hand. "Take this time away, and you can apologize when you come home. You'd be surprised how far an apology can go toward forgiveness."

"People don't forgive the boogeymen under their beds, Mother. You should know that better than anyone —you tried to unalive yours." I make a stabbing motion with my fist, and she recoils like she's horrified I'd be crass enough to bring it up. Rolling my eyes, I bark out a mocking laugh. "Daddy was a monster. You know it, I know it, and that's what he made me. I endured eighteen years of his hell—his lies, distorted reality, and need for vengeance."

Using every mental and physical degradation at his disposal, he molded me into his perfect weapon—beautiful, malicious, deviously spiteful, and broken as fuck. Meant to marry the Halliday heir and secure my father unfettered access to destroy the families who shunned him from within.

Until I found out that none of what he'd worked so hard to make me believe was real.

I learned his depraved cruelty extended far beyond

me when the truth about what he did to Catherine Bradley came to light that night. That his entire made-up world had sprouted from jealousy and greed, cultivated in a garden of darkness and evil planted by his own dirty hands. Hearing my father recount the atrocities and incredible acts of violence he committed with a sick and twisted pride was disgusting.

"Hali, please."

Something in her voice forces me to sneak a sideways glance her way. The reference to my father sends a ripple of revulsion through her shiny, new, not-a-victim persona. For half a second, the dish rag I remember from my childhood peeks through, and she goes blank. She recovers quickly, smoothing her hair with a hand showing only the slightest tremor.

"Please what? Please pretend I don't have a half-sister I knew nothing about until this year? Pretend Daddy had nothing to do with the tragic, short, life of *her* mother? Or wait, pretend you didn't lose your fucking mind and stab him with a broken martini glass in front of a roomful of people? Hell, that's the only thing I've ever respected you for so that one's getting added to the family scrapbook."

I'm still dumbfounded at the lack of a trial, or jury, after that night. Obscenely well-paid lawyers swooped in, expert mental health practitioners in tow. Between them and the unlimited coffers of the founding families, no charges were laid. Eleanor's attempt to end my father's life was deemed a combination of self-defense, provocation, and diminished capacity. Instead of prison, she was carted off to a treatment facility in the wilds of Oregon for a 'rest'.

Dear old Dad survived the jagged chunk of glass she jammed into his neck, but after being in an induced coma for a few weeks, his shriveled, black heart quit. At least, that's the official story. I wouldn't be surprised if somebody kinked his oxygen tube or injected an air bubble into his IV—hell, I wouldn't blame them. Callum Torsten was the devil and deserved every bad thing that ever happened to him and more.

"You'll be fine. You're nothing like him."

It's like everything I just said was sucked into a vacuum—a black hole of denial and dismissal. Her tone rings with uncertainty, though, and I pounce on it.

"You don't know a damn thing about me, Eleanor. You never have. The only reason we're even in this car right now is because that grizzled old windbag at school decided to squeal."

The summons to the headmistress's office comes during third-period English. The irritation I feel at being called out of class is nothing compared to when I round the corner and spot Eleanor standing in the hall. Or a reasonable facsimile of her anyway.

From my earliest memories, my mother may as well have been a ghost. Mostly mute and dismally drab, both in looks and demeanor, she showed no evidence of a backbone to call her own. But the woman talking to Sunday Easton and Stella Bradleigh is anything but drab.

She sparkles. Gone is the fog of misery and the dense, gray, nothingness of depression. Instead of her usual dank, straw-like hair, and meek, cowed expression, she's resplendent in a cobalt dress, her hair styled in shining, dark waves. A dazzling smile creases her full and delicately pinked cheeks.

Some weird mom radar thing must alert her to my presence, and her gaze turns razor-sharp. Through tight lips, she curtly informs me we're both required to meet with the headmistress of Woodington Academy. Stunned by her appearance and the unexpected stab of hurt that she didn't bother to tell me she was coming home, I've got no words. I simply trail behind her into the office.

Faye Gillies has been a harridan since the dawn of time. A dried-up old woman, fifty years past her prime, she's bitter and butthurt at the hand life dealt her. She's earned herself a reputation of moral superiority at Woodington and developed an iron fist to go along with her high horse.

In her spacious office that reeks of heavy floral potpourri and old money, that fist punched me right in the stomach.

"Thank you for coming, Mrs. Torsten. I'd like to share a few things about your daughter with you."

While my mother was busy forgetting she had a kid, Ms. Gillies was compiling a nice, fat file of my wrongdoings.

Years' worth of them. Sitting across from the unpleasant woman with her pinched features and raggedy steel wool hair, I swear glee shines from her eyes as she rattles off a litany of my transgressions. By the time the old bat is finished, even I have the good sense to be mortified by the picture she painted.

My mother's face is tight, the pink of her cheeks now a bright crimson. The calm with which she pronounces my fate is admirable, especially since my stomach drops straight out of my ass at her decree.

"I'm pulling Hali from Woodington Academy effective immediately. This is not a suitable environment for her. She will be attending a residential therapy program in northern Washington state."

My anxiety ranks somewhere in the vicinity of a sweaty, clueless teenage boy in desperate search of his girlfriend's clit.

In the dark.

On speed.

Good old Faye gave my mother the perfect excuse to make her most significant reminder of my father disappear. The emotions boiling under my surface are impossible for me to describe, partly because at least three of them I don't recognize.

Nobody discusses my future or asks me what I want. Instead, I get a one-way plane ticket and a different parent controlling my life for their own ends.

Since Eleanor announced her decision, I'd refused to give her the satisfaction of acknowledging she existed. It wasn't difficult—she'd been absent for most of my life, even though she slept in the bedroom down the hall.

That wall of silence between us held until the dickhead at the airport cut the line at the coffee place. The black hoodie he wore obscured most of his face, but the angle of his jaw and the arrogant set of his sexy lips screamed bad boy. On most days, I'd find that hot. Today it irritated the shit out of me.

Piping up with her chastising comment about my language, Eleanor dumped a barrel of gasoline on an already significant fire. It took everything in me to hold back the seventeen derivatives of 'fuck' I wanted to spew at her just to watch her head explode.

And now I've been stuck in this damn car with her for over two hours.

"It's not fair of you to say I don't know you, Hali. I never—"

"*Not fair*? Are you kidding me? You want to talk about not fair, Mommy Dearest?"

The car rolls to a smooth stop and she should count her lucky stars she's been spared the white-hot force of my rage.

Our driver lowers the privacy divider and announces we've arrived, and I get my first good look at The Overlook. The main building of the ridiculous 'wellness retreat' is a somewhat squat structure constructed of heavy gray stone and weathered wood and framed by tall cedars. A handful of small bungalows peek through the trees on either side, and the whole place looks a little like a horror movie waiting to happen.

"Picked up a little blood lust after Daddy, huh? Sending me off to be ax-murdered and out of your hair for good, too?"

"Stop being so dramatic, please." The woman who gave me life but little else presses her forefingers to her temples and squeezes her eyes shut. "This is far more difficult for me than you seem to think."

"How exactly is this difficult for *you*? How does this have anything to do with you?" My voice is controlled, belying none of the rage and fear thickening my blood. "How long do I have to stay here?"

"Nobody's forcing you to stay anywhere. If you want to walk away, go ahead. But I've got control of the purse strings until you're twenty-one, and I promise you you'll leave with nothing." She sighs, the sound cold and put-upon. "This is the best place for you right now, Hali. The initial program here is four weeks long. After that, we'll talk. The change of scenery will do you good."

"And keep me from inconveniencing you." The words drip with an acid that burns my tongue.

"Maybe I don't want you to carry the damage he inflicted on you for the rest of your life." The sentiment is noticeably hollow and makes me want to punch her.

"You did nothing to stop it then," I point out, my fingers unconsciously seeking out the smooth, silver, teardrop pendant weighing around my neck. Not looking at her, I keep my tone bland and bored. "So, you'll have to excuse me if what you want now means jack shit to me."

My gaze tracks a willowy young woman in faded jeans and an oatmeal-colored cable-knit sweater as she laughs at somebody over her shoulder. Letting the door swing shut behind her, she crosses the wide front porch and starts down the stairs, her long golden blonde waves undulating in the breeze like she just walked out of a shampoo commercial.

"Hali, I can say I'm sorry for everything that happened, but I can't be the one to help you." Her voice turns rock hard and determined, allowing zero room for argument. "Make no mistake, daughter dear, I will not have the seeds your father planted in your psyche ripening into twisted, rotting fruit. You've done some awful things in your young life, and the road you're on leads nowhere good. You want the money he left you? You want your privileged life back? Then this is where you need to be." She softens slightly. "This is your chance to choose a different path—one that wasn't paved by him. A chance at something new."

The frightened little girl buried deep within me rattles the bars of her cage at the idea of a fresh start. That part of me wants nothing more than for my mom to hug me and tell me no matter how many horrible things I've done, she loves me. But true to form, neither the hug nor the words materialize, and the acrimony takes hold again. My fingers stop fidgeting with my long necklace, and I reach for the door handle.

The chill air engulfs me as soon as I step out of the car, cooling the burn of my unshed tears. The trees and the Sound combine into an unfamiliar, almost intoxicating scent, filling my lungs and senses. Taking a deep breath, I exhale through pursed lips and turn back to face the woman still seated in the depths of the town car.

"No need to step out, Mother. You can keep your platitudes and shove them straight up your ass." The words are sand in my throat, dusty and dry. Slamming the door on any response she might have, I grab the two suitcases the driver retrieves from the trunk. Their hot pink hard shells mock me, looking much more suited to a holiday on a tropical island than a stay in a glorified mental hospital.

Oatmeal sweater girl reaches the car and offers her hand.

"Hi, Hali, I'm Mari. Can I help you with your bags?" Up close, she's younger than I first thought and comes across as sincere enough, but I'm pissed off at the world today, and that includes her.

"All good, Mari," I answer, my trademark smirk firmly in place. "Let's just get this over with, m'kay?"

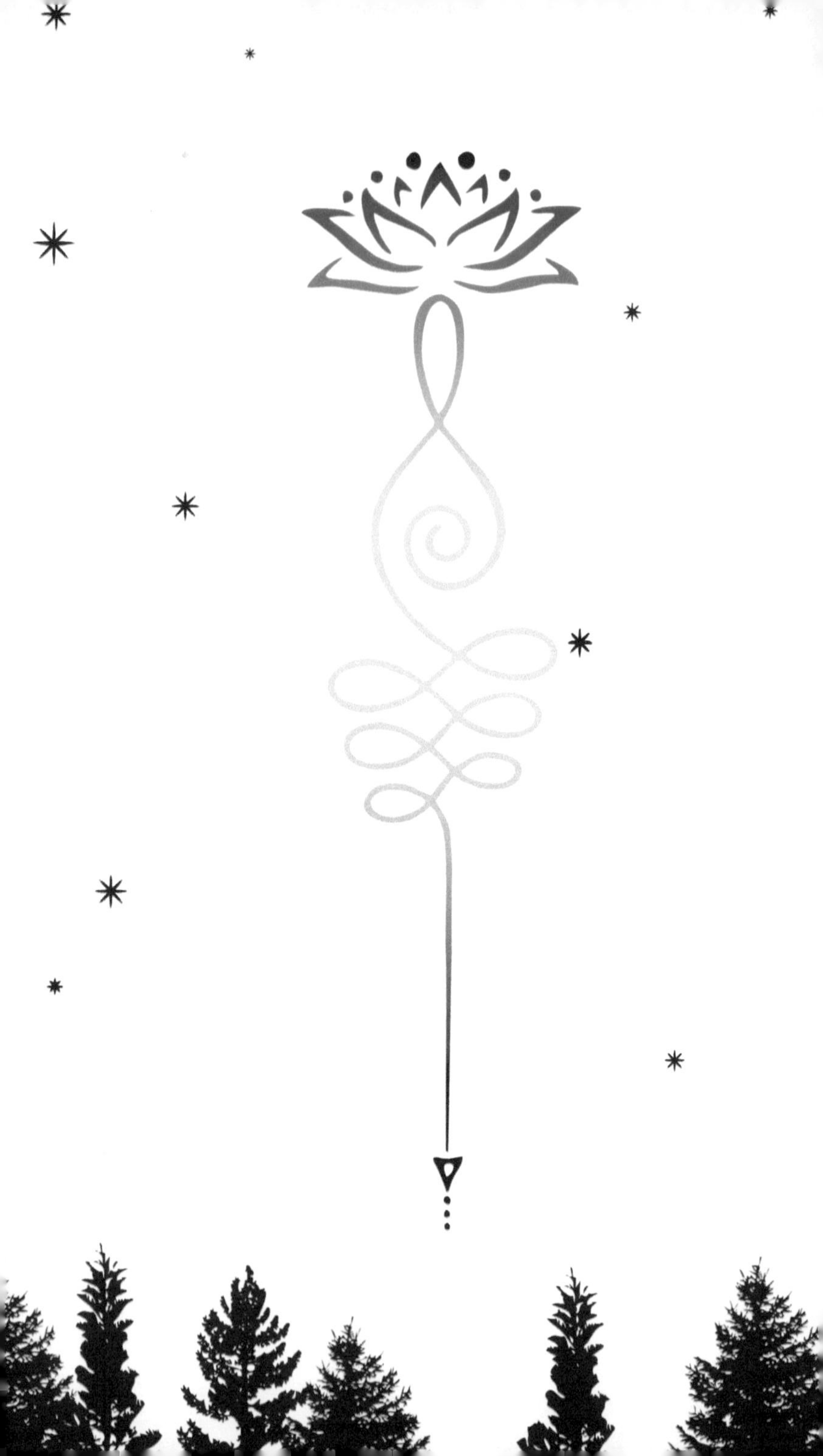

CHAPTER FIVE

Hali

Mari steps aside, lips twitching, and gestures ahead of her with an exaggerated sweep of her arm. I flip my hair and stomp my way up the stairs and through the enormous front door, tugging my bags along with me.

If I was in a better mood, I'd appreciate the deep leather couches, flagstone fireplace big enough to walk into, and expansive windows. In my current state of mind, however, the interior is cloying and claustrophobic and rubs my nose in the cozy, loving family I never had. Even the lingering traces of lavender and woodsmoke are so traditionally homey that they make me nauseous.

"This is the lodge. All therapy sessions, group or otherwise, are held in this building, along with your self-directed learning," Mari explains. "Group is coed and led by yours truly, while individual therapists are assigned based on the guests' needs and the best fit."

"You're a shrink?" I ask, surprised. "How old are you, twelve?"

"Not a shrink, a psychologist," she corrects. "I don't prescribe. As for my age, that's none of your business, so 'old enough' will have to do." The hint of snark frames her in a slightly different light than my initial impression of a granola-crunching hippie. Vague curiosity replaces some of my disdain.

"How many inmates are here?" I try in vain to force both suitcases to roll evenly on either side of me instead of banging into my calves.

"We prefer to call you 'guests' since 'inmates' tends to look bad on a brochure," her response is thick with sarcasm. "Eleven, including you." She lets me struggle for a few more seconds. "Don't like to ask for help much, huh?" Reaching for the handle of the smaller case, she tugs it free of my fingers.

"I've never had anyone to ask," I mumble as we make our way to the double doors on the far side of the large room.

The look she shoots me stinks of sympathy, which she can shove straight up her skinny ass, but it's colored by something else too, something knowing.

What exactly has my mother told her? How much of our family tea did she spill?

"Down this hall," she points to the corridor that runs

the length of one wing, "are the staff offices. When a therapist is assigned to you, that's where you'll meet for your one-on-one sessions." Twisting, she points toward the opposite wing. "Cafeteria and infirmary are that way, along with a well-equipped gym and a washroom with showers and lockers. Lunch is served buffet style every day between noon and two, and drinks and snacks are available from six a.m. to midnight. Any medical issues or concerns, the infirmary is staffed twenty-four hours." She turns to push through the doors.

Whoa. What? Concerns? Oh, I have a fucking concern.

"Back the hell up. *Lunch* is served every day? What happened to breakfast and dinner?"

She just grins and shoves through the doors, leaving me staring after her, suspicious and confused.

One meal a day? What kind of cheap-ass place did my mother stick me in?

"Better hurry, love. Don't want to get lost." An elderly woman with an ID lanyard around her neck pipes up from behind the enormous cherrywood desk near the front door. The realization that she's right doesn't stop me from shooting her a dirty look, but it does make my feet move.

The back of the lodge is far more interesting than the front. From this vantage point, the view out over Puget Sound is breathtaking. Not visible from the road, the entire back of the property slopes gently down to a beach that's more pebbles than sand. In the distance, a white ferry smoothly cuts toward a thickly forested island, and the sound of the water kissing the shore plays with the occasional calls of the gulls.

"Pretty, isn't it?" Mari waits just outside the exit.

"Sure, whatever," I snipe, dismissing her attempt to start an actual conversation. There's no way I'm letting on to some stranger that the constant tangle of knots in my stomach is noticeably looser since I stepped out of the car. "Just finish the damn tour and show me my room."

She gives me a mock salute and starts walking.

"We have seven cabins here, with room for two guests in each. Five are full now that you're here, one is empty, and the last one is occupied by another new arrival who has requested private quarters."

"Cabins? Like, *cabins* cabins?" Deepening dread ratchets up my bitchiness. "Great, it's a demented summer camp for crazies." I feign snot-nosed innocence. "Does The Overlook supply the butcher knives and hockey masks, or were we supposed to bring our own?"

Until now, Mari has ignored my shitty attitude or made light of my snide comments, but not this time—this time, she comes to a full stop.

"Make jokes about yourself all you want, Hali, if that's what you need to do to cope." She turns to face me, authoritative without raising her voice. "But do not think for one second that I or any other staff member will tolerate you mocking, belittling, or bullying the other guests. 'Crazy' is not a term we use around here. These people came to The Overlook for help; the last thing they need is a spoiled brat making fun of them. Do you understand?" We have a bit of a stare-down until I'm compelled to break eye contact.

"Yeah, sure," I answer quietly, looking at my shoes.

Frustration and embarrassment war for dominance, and both piss me off. Growing up, my father drilled into my head that embarrassment is weak, and weaklings end up cast away by society to rot in a corner.

Maybe he was right.

Maybe this place is just one big ol' corner that Eleanor dumped me in.

Maybe I deserve it.

I shake my head to clear the niggling little voice that sounds way too much like a dead man's. Striding after Mari, I catch up with her at the door of a cabin that faces the water.

"This is where you'll be staying while you're with us. Your bunkmate is in a private session but will be here to meet you as soon as she's done. There's a bedroom and bathroom, a small living room, gas fireplace, and full kitchen stocked with plates, glasses, silv—"

"I'm sorry, why is a kitchen a selling feature?" I cut her off sharply, putting two and two together and hoping it equals something other than four.

"We offer a shuttle into town twice a week to pick up groceries and any personal items you might need. You are responsible for your own breakfasts and dinners, as well as for keeping the cabin tidy and cleaning up after yourself. Any other questions?" Her voice is calm in the face of my mounting freak-out.

"*Any other questions?*" Panic blooms in the pit of my stomach. "What in the holy hell is going on? There's no way my mother paid for the self-serve option. Do I strike you as somebody who can cook?" My eyes widen, and my voice pitches an octave or two higher than usual, making her laugh wryly.

"Your mother knew what she was paying for, and that we don't offer any other option. If you want to eat, you'd better learn your way around a kitchen, huh?" With those unhelpful words, she deposits my small suitcase at my feet and turns back toward the lodge. "Welcome to The Overlook, Hali," she calls over her shoulder before breaking into a jog and leaving me staring after her open-mouthed.

Before I can swallow it, an angry shriek stretches my vocal cords, and I stamp my foot on the tiny verandah like a five-year-old. Pissed off, stressed out, and disoriented, I throw the cabin door wide open and stalk into my temporary home, dragging my suitcases behind me. When the smaller one slams into my ankle bone for the seventeenth time, I haul off and punt it into the middle of the living room. It falls over on its side and lays there silently judging me.

Fuck it. Fuck this place. Fuck my mother. Fuck Mari.

Fuck learning to cook. And fuck the fact that I'm sweating like a whore in church. Why is it a million degrees in here?

I cross my arms and grab the hem of my thick sweater in both hands, but when I try to pull it off, it tangles with my long necklace and longer hair. My vicious yanking does nothing except make it worse. Unable to hold my tongue, the frustration of the superbly shitty day spews out in a run-on sentence made entirely of curse words and guttural grunts.

With a final screech, I fight my way out of the knot of sweater and necklace trying to smother me and fling it all across the room. The heavy silver pendant clatters to the floor as the knit material puddles around it like a sigh. Standing in the middle of the small room in my tank top and jeans, sweaty and out of breath, my cheeks burn when a masculine-sounding throat clears behind me. I freeze, grinding my teeth behind lips clamped tight.

Fantastic. Of course, I have an audience. Can this day get any worse?

I tilt my head back to stare at the ceiling, breath blowing out in a rush while I pray for the patience not to strangle my uninvited guest. Then, with a last huff, I turn and get an eyeful of the witness to my tantrum.

Tall, lean, and broad-shouldered, he looks a few years older than me. Lounging against the front door frame, he devours me with arresting steel gray eyes. Dark hair, tousled either by the breeze or by design, adds a layer of disheveled sexiness to his already magnetically attractive features. Every ripple and dip of sculpted chest and tapered waist is emphasized by his charcoal thermal Henley, while the sleeves pushed up his forearms reveal tendrils of intricate ink. He cocks an eyebrow and grins raunchily at my open perusal.

"Hungry?" he asks, notes of smoke and grit and sex in his voice.

"Huh?" My brain fights its way out of my panties and yanks me back to attention. "Hungry? What? No. Why?"

"You're salivating, little girl. I'd be happy to oblige if you need something to eat." He casually slides one hand down over the washboard hinted at through his fitted shirt, until he gets to his crotch. Then, without breaking eye contact, he grabs his dick suggestively.

I stifle the involuntary shudder of revulsion that ripples through my soul at his use of my father's favorite pet name.

'Little girl'? Oh, hell no. Nobody calls me 'little girl' anymore. Today is not the day, and I am not the one, motherfucker.

I tilt my head to the side and squint my eyes appraisingly in the direction of the prominent bulge in his slim-fitting black jeans.

"Not sure that would be much of a meal." I tap my lower lip thoughtfully with a manicured nail. "I mean, really?" I move my hand and wave a dismissive gesture toward his zipper. "That's more like one of those little finger sandwiches they serve at afternoon tea. You know," contempt drips from my words, "the ones that do nothing to satisfy you and just leave you hungry for a real meal?" I shrug one shoulder and choke back a victorious cackle as he pulls himself up to his entire six foot two or three, radiating righteous indignation tinged with just a hint of shock.

"Sweetheart, a stuck-up rich girl like you wouldn't know what to do with what I'm packing. I'd split you in two," he threatens, all bruised masculinity.

"Not without bringing an ax to bed, you wouldn't," I assure him, studying my fingernails in feigned boredom.

His immediate response, somewhere between a chuckle and growl, dampens the scrap of lace between my legs.

Damn, this guy is sexy as fuck. Too bad he's such a prick.

With Herculean effort, I try to keep my gaze frosty as I lift my eyes to meet his. The silent power struggle balloons around us, heavy with innuendo and challenge.

"Oh, taking you down a few pegs is going to be so much fun." A cruel smirk slides over his lips. His narrowed eyes can't hide the anticipation that flashes in them, like lightning racing through thunderclouds. He waits for a few more beats, broody and delicious, before turning and casually strolling away.

All the air seems to flood back into the room at once, leaving me lightheaded and momentarily dazed.

Before I can collect myself, the space he vacated is occupied by a pretty Asian girl who gawks at me.

"What the hell do you want?" I snap rudely, and she raises her perfect jet-black eyebrows in surprise.

"I live here," she answers like I just asked her the most ridiculous question ever. Grabbing the door frame with both hands, she leans back to look outside. Satisfied that we're alone, she focuses on me again, jerking her thumb in the direction of my unwelcome visitor's exit. "What was *he* doing here?"

"Annoying me? Being a douchebag? Take your pick." I roll my eyes, and it makes me painfully aware of the migraine brewing behind them.

"Don't you know who he is? You don't, do you?" Her voice drips with astonishment. Like the fact that I don't recognize Mr. Arrogant Man Meat is beyond human comprehension.

I shake my head in response and rub my temples, hoping this ridiculous conversation ends quickly so I can find my bed and crawl into it. Or under it.

"Ty McInnis?" she says, and I stare blankly back at her. "Tyler Draven McInnis, the front man for Heroin Heartbreak?"

The band name sounds familiar, but I'm pissy right now and refuse to give her the satisfaction, so I shrug my shoulders dismissively.

"Good Lord, we need to educate you because either you've been living in a cultural vacuum, or you have terrible taste in music. Every female under the age of sixty knows who Ty McInnis is." She steps into the cabin and shuts the door behind her. "I'm your bunkmate, by the way. Vannessa Yi, but most people call me Vann. The ones that acknowledge me anyway." She sticks out a hand.

When all I do is eyeball it like a dead fish, she awkwardly drops it back to her side. The uncomfortable purse of her lips has me relenting for some reason.

"Hali Torsten," is all I offer, but you'd think I'd given her my entire life story, the way it perks her back up.

"Nice to meet you." She shoots me a lopsided grin and trots to the fridge to pull out a small bottle of Diet Coke. Scraping back one of the two chairs on opposite sides of the little dining table, she drops into it. Her small, delicate hands twist her long, inky black hair into a sleek ponytail, and she snaps a hair tie off her wrist to secure it. "So, don't leave me hanging. What did Ty want? It's not every day you meet a legit rock star." She pauses. "I wonder what it'll be like having him here. I mean, is he going to be an attention whore, trying to get the gir—"

"He offered to let me suck his dick."

Vann's eyes bug as she chokes and sputters on her saliva, and she coughs. Before she can recover, I continue.

"Look, can we play the get-to-know-you game later?

I'm drained and just want to put my shit away and take a shower."

"Oh, yeah, sorry." She looks disappointed but nods and jumps up, leaving the unopened bottle of soda on the table. Before I can stop her, she grabs the handle of my toppled suitcase on her way through the living room. I lag a few steps behind, dragging the larger case with me. "The bathroom is at the end of the hall, and this is the bedroom." Vann parks my luggage at the foot of a stripped bed.

Besides the fact that the mattress is small as hell, the room itself isn't as bad as I expected. With decent-sized windows on two walls, it's large enough to hold doubles of everything—single beds, tall dressers, and small nightstands—and still have plenty of space to move. Soft dove gray walls compliment the polished wood floors, highlighted by the dappled afternoon light filtering through the trees outside.

My new roomie retrieves a neatly folded pile of sheets, blankets, and a bath towel from one side of the closet and deposits it all in my arms.

"Here you go. I'll leave you alone to organize your stuff. If you need anything, just holler. This is going to be so great." She leans in and gives me a quick hug, the stack of linens getting squished between us.

I stand frozen, unaccustomed to such an overt display of affection and totally uncomfortable with it.

Ignoring the awkward situation, Vann bounces out of the room, enthusiasm recharged.

Shell-shocked, confused, and emotionally wrecked, I drop everything except the towel on the mattress. Auto-pilot kicks in, and I grab a change of clothes and the toiletry case from my bag before walking down the hall to the bathroom. After thumbing the small lock under the doorknob, I turn on the faucet in the sink full blast and sit heavily on the bathtub's edge.

Thankful for a few moments of privacy, I grip the white porcelain, fingers rigid and cold. My composure folds in on itself, and the sound of the rushing water drowns out the sobs I never let anybody hear.

Half an hour later, outwardly composed and freshly showered, I twist my wet hair into a sloppy braid and dig out my moisturizer. The rich cream scented faintly of roses is cool on my skin, and the slow circular motions I use to apply it are almost hypnotic in my exhausted state.

Unpacking is the last thing on the planet I want to do right now, but my father's whispers in the back of my mind spur me to do it anyway. His punishments when things were out of place left mental scars far worse than any that ever showed on my skin.

The memories bleed across my features, and rage-tinted fear lights my eyes with an eerie, hollow glow. Unable to face my reflection any longer, I shove everything back in the travel case and scoop up my discarded clothes from the floor. My footsteps back to the bedroom are heavy and slow, the array of emotions coursing through me like shackles around my ankles.

The larger of my suitcases holds the limited clothing options I brought—just enough to take up half the dresser and even less of my side of the shared closet. Angry packing isn't my strong suit, and the wardrobe choices I've left myself with reflect that. Shaking my head at the glittery silver camisole hanging next to soft hoodies and one of my navy plaid school skirts, I can't help a whispered *'what the actual fuck?'* I unzip the smaller suitcase and toss the assorted shoes and boots inside the bottom of the closet.

In under five minutes I'm done. Usually, being alone in the quiet for this long would be enough to trigger my anxiety. I don't remember the last time I've been comfortable in my own company. The silence here hits differently, though—it still whispers, but more of possibilities than accusations.

Wrung out after the whirlwind of the past two days, my shoulders sag on a heavy sigh, and the headache that was only a maybe earlier blossoms into a certainty. The stark white mattress, even without bedding, is the most inviting thing I've seen in months. It's surprisingly soft when I curl up on my side, and I cautiously allow my mind to drift, something I don't often indulge in. Control is usually a necessity for me. My dark corners are filled with lurking horrors that require near-constant mental pressure to keep from tearing me apart.

Letting my gaze wander around the unfamiliar room, a sense of peace descends over me.

There's nothing here to remind me. Maybe I really can start over.

The sun has moved lower in the sky, causing the mosaic created by the convergence of light and trees to climb from the floor to the wall. Entranced by the dancing patterns, I watch until my eyelids grow heavy with sleep.

CHAPTER SIX

Hali

I have no idea what time it is when I surface from my much-needed snooze. My lids are closed, but I can somehow sense the room is empty. As if on cue, Vann's voice increases in volume as she comes down the hall, reaching me before she does.

"Hey, Hali, do you want to g—" She stops short in the doorway. "Oh, sorry, I didn't know you were napping." Her tone turns apologetic and slightly disappointed.

Sure, I could lie here and pretend to be still asleep, but my stomach is loudly protesting the lack of any real food today. And the crazy cook-your-own-damn-dinner policy means I need to ask for help scrounging something to eat. The thought of asking anybody for anything in this place gives me hives. Sighing, I sit up and stretch the kinks out of my neck and shoulders.

"I'm awake. What's up?"

"You want to go walk around a bit? Maybe grab a snack in the cafeteria?"

Wow, that was easy. I didn't even have to ask.

"Food. God, yes, I'm ravenous. Just let me grab a sweater." Crossing to the closet, I reach for my favorite soft pink Roxy hoodie.

"What's that mean?" I turn and catch her gesturing with a finger swirl to the delicate tattoo partially exposed by my racerback tank. The black ink runs vertically down the length of my left shoulder blade, disappearing under my shirt.

"It's the Unalome. Symbolizes the path to enlightenment." After pulling on my sweater, I look up from the zipper and catch the tail-end of her surprised expression before she has a chance to hide it. "What?" I ask defensively, prepared to kibosh the whole foraging for snacks idea and starve to death rather than have this stranger make fun of me. "You have a problem with my tattoo?"

"Not at all." She grins. "It's beautiful. I just didn't expect it to mean something so...grown-up, I guess? Most of the kids back home got theirs on a whim. You know, the same market flash that seven thousand other people have."

Rolling her eyes, she pulls on a hoodie of her own. "One of them got these kanji on her forearm. Told everybody they meant loyalty, love, and luck. On a class trip to Japan last year, the locals would snicker every time she wore a short sleeve shirt. I asked a server at our hotel restaurant why and she explained they were laughing at the clueless American with the silly ink. It turns out her tattoo actually means 'three person woman." She laughs, a ridiculous noise, brash and hee-hawing.

"Given she was sleeping with most of the football team at the time, it was perfect for her," she gets out before dissolving into another fit of giggles. The sound must be contagious because I'm staring at her like she's lost her marbles one minute and laughing right along with her the next.

When we finally stop to catch our breath, my sides are aching, and my cheeks hurt. Out of nowhere, it hits me that I can't remember the last time that happened, and I'm instantly somber. Snotty snickers and catty chuckles don't count. Removing all of those, I don't think I've laughed in years.

What's the matter with me? Who the hell doesn't laugh? Damaged girls with severe daddy issues, that's who.

"Hey, Hali, you okay? Where'd you go just then?" Vann snaps her fingers in front of my face, all traces of humor erased.

"What? Oh. Yeah, I'm fine." I shake it off and busy my hands with smoothing my braid. "Ready when you are."

She side-eyes me like she might push the issue, but something in my expression must tell her now's not the time, and she shifts gears.

"Not to be a pain, but we should probably do something about that before we go anywhere." She gestures to the naked mattress. "Having to do it later when you're ready to go to bed will suck."

"Uh, sure."

There's not a snowball's chance of me admitting I've never put sheets on a bed before. That's always been the housekeeper's job. My ineptitude must be a flashing neon sign on my forehead, though, because she takes the lead. Without a single hint of condescension, she teaches me how to make something she calls hospital corners with the top sheet. We throw the bright, multi-colored comforter over the whole thing when we're done, and grab our phones.

My new roomie is a walking tabloid, dropping tidbits about the other guests like gossipy breadcrumbs as we walk up the path to the main lodge. It's so overwhelming that by the time we slip through the back doors, I've already forgotten at least half of what she said.

Our footsteps echo softly in the deserted building, and we both fall silent on the way to the cafeteria. I'm grateful the place is empty—the fewer people to deal with, the better. And in a similarly pleasant development, once inside the large, comfortably furnished room, I realize Mari neglected to mention that 'snacks' covers everything from potato chips to fresh fruit and sandwiches.

I choose two blueberry muffins, each easily twice the size of my fist, and a bright red apple. Vann pulls a green glass bottle out of the glass-doored refrigerated cooler for each of us. We flop down at a table near the windows, and she swaps me a fizzy water for a baked good.

The only sounds in the softly lit room are the tap-tap-tap of tree branches against the windows as they sway with the breeze in the gathering dark.

"It's not exactly dinner, but at least it's something." Vann breaks the silence apologetically.

"Best muffin ever," I mumble with my mouth full, and she laughs.

"We can do better tomorrow. It's shuttle day, so we can go into town and stock up on groceries."

"About that..." Before I can grill her about the whole cooking our own meals thing, the sound of increasingly loud, raucous laughter warns us we're about to have company.

As I drain the last of my water, three guys stroll in, and stop briefly inside the cafeteria doors. All in their early twenties, they survey the room with the cocky entitlement reserved for the insanely wealthy or the ridiculously hot. I can't speak to the size of their bank accounts, but they definitely meet the looks criteria. Two of them look surprised to find us here, but the third, not so much.

The predatory grin curving Ty's lips makes me

wonder if he knew exactly who he'd find here tonight. Considering his supposed fame, I consult what I remember of the mental map Vann drew for me. I'm almost positive Ty is the one who requested private digs and that those digs are in the cabin next to ours. The naturally suspicious part of me thinks maybe he decided to follow us.

They move as a unit first to the refrigerated coolers then, drinks in hand, to a group of comfy-looking chairs in the corner closest to us. Their intent to stay and hang out for a while quickly becomes evident, and while I'm not thrilled with them being here, that's not my biggest issue.

Ty is.

Every time I shift my eyes in their direction, he's glaring back at me. The animosity rolling off him in waves floods the space between us and I can't figure out why it annoys me so much. It's like he hates me without knowing who I am. Truth be told, that's nothing new in my world, but something about this guy has me on edge.

Doing our best to ignore the unwelcome company, Vann and I continue our conversation, but it's difficult. Their presence is distracting, and they're fully aware of it. Every so often, a burst of laughter erupts that's a little too loud, laced with snark and mockery. The kind of laugh designed to get our attention.

The force of her disapproval carves a sharp furrow between Vann's brows, but something else flits briefly across her features as well. It's gone before I can give it a name, though, and the disapproval is back in full force.

"Talk about small dick energy," she mutters. "All ego and 'look at me, look at me' crap."

"I can't speak for the other two, but I'm pretty sure there's nothing small about Ty's dick, metaphorically or otherwise." I punctuate my reply with a shrug.

Vann's response, somewhere between that donkey laugh of hers and the harsh cough of a two-pack-a-day smoker, draws three sets of eyes directly to us.

I spin around and face them head-on, my practiced smirk in full effect. Then, bringing the tips of both middle fingers to my lips, I kiss them lightly before offering them up in salute. The two guys I haven't met burst into laughter, but Ty's glare gets even darker.

What the fuck is with this guy?

Vann returns to her grumbling.

"Seriously, Hali, guys are so dumb. Why do they think acting like arrogant assholes will get them any attention?"

Because it will.

I'm familiar with the tactic since it's long been a weapon in my own arsenal. Being on the receiving end of it for a change is pissing me off, though, and the old Hali—the one I'd love to put behind me—is itching to come out and play. Resistance is becoming more difficult by the second. The longer Ty bores holes in my back with his stormy gray eyes, the more I want to scratch them out. If I don't get up and walk away, things will turn really ugly, really quick, and any hope of this being a fresh start for me will disappear.

I raise an eyebrow at my roommate, hoping she can decipher my non-verbal cue, and thankfully she answers with a nearly imperceptible nod. The two of us grab our garbage and empty bottles and dump it all in the trash and recycling bins at the door. Our imminent departure does nothing to ease the tension hanging in the room— if anything, it does the opposite, and I'm not sticking around to find out why.

CHAPTER SEVEN

Ty

What are the odds? Not only is she here, but she's right fucking next door.

Curiosity got the better of me when the unholy shriek reverberated from the cabin beside mine. When I sidled up to the door, the sight that greeted me had me biting back my first true urge to laugh in months. With her back to me, she lifted her face toward the ceiling and her long thick hair touched her superb ass.

Something about that visual made my dick twitch and when she turned to face me, I recognized her instantly. The same can't be said for her, though. Sure, I had my hoodie pulled all the way up, purposely shadowing my face at the coffee shop, but come on. If you're going to spill a guy's coffee and try to crush his foot, I figure you should at least recognize him when you're face to face again a few hours later.

Women.

"Oooof," the out-of-breath cutie with glossy, jet-black, hair exclaims as I round the corner and plow straight into her.

"Shit. Sorry about that."

The shock written all over her face tells me *she* recognizes me. I flash her an apologetic grin and a pink flush spreads high on her cheeks before she scurries away toward the cabin I just left.

Alone on the path again, I'm right back in my head. The girl next door got under my skin without trying from the moment she opened her mouth at the coffee shop. I don't remember the last time I had such an immediate and instinctual reaction to anybody. If I'm honest, I don't know that I've *ever* had one.

The whole thing irritates the hell out of me.

Her snarky comebacks.

Her attitude.

Her curves.

I shouldn't be reacting to her the way I am, and I sure as hell refuse to let her in on how much she's affecting me.

This time away is a chance to be completely selfish and not have to worry about anybody else for once. An opportunity to grieve and get my head on straight. Now is not the time to be caught up in pussy, perfect tits, and an attitude that begs to be broken.

Back in my own cabin, I chug a large glass of ice

water, but it does little to cool the heat pulsing through my veins. I strip down and jump in the shower, and thankfully, the water pressure here is better than in most high-end hotels. I stand under the powerful spray and let it wash away my burgeoning hard-on, the scent of spilled coffee, and the memory of the bluest eyes I've ever seen.

S howered and changed, my growling stomach and a need for distraction take precedence. I'm on my way up to the cafeteria in the main lodge when a familiar voice rings out.

"Yo, McInnis! What the fuck are you doing here?" Miles Felhaber leans in for a bro hug. "Need a break from being a big shot?"

"Here for a little maintenance is all." I laugh, unwilling to let on how close to the truth he is. "What about you?"

Miles was a client here during my last stay, too. While not what I would consider a good friend by any stretch, we had some laughs, which made things a little easier for both of us last time.

"Got caught with a noseful of blow by my old man."

"That's it? One snow white transgression hardly qualifies as an Overlook-level offense."

"Might've had something to do with me being balls

deep in my stepmother at the time and snorting the lines off her big, fake tits." He laughs, and his buddy slaps him appreciatively on the back.

"Yeah, okay, that would do it."

Inwardly, I cringe. These wealthy brats show up here all entitled and bragging about the stupid shit they do, proving that money doesn't buy class. Hell, Kess has more of it in his left nut than these idiots do in their whole bodies, and he spent most of his life not having two nickels to rub together.

"Oh." He jerks his thumb toward the guy beside him. "This is Marino. Marino, this is Ty McInnis, world-famous pussy-magnet."

"S'up." Marino acknowledges me with a typical frat boy chin flick while Miles nods toward the cabin behind me.

"Mari hooked you up with the same shack as last time, huh?"

"Yeah, she did. Where are you bunking?"

"We're over on the other side. The cabin next to ours houses a couple of hotties if you're looking for a little action." He chuckles lecherously and punches me in the shoulder. "Hey, we're heading to the lodge to grab something from the cafeteria. You coming?"

Since I was already heading that way, I shrug and fall in with them. Unfortunately, the conversation all the way up the path is on the level of dick and fart jokes, making me regret my decision to tag along.

That all changes when we walk in and approach the cafeteria. The voices inside are quiet but still discernible with the double doors propped open, and I can tell exactly who it is. As soon as the other two cross the threshold and catch sight of her sitting with the girl who nearly ran me over earlier, they stop in their tracks.

"Holy shit," Miles says under his breath.

"Which one?" I ask the question already knowing his answer.

"That one," he nods. "The one with the braid."

"Yeah, she's hot, but she's also a bitch," I warn.

"The bitchy ones have teeth. I like teeth. You call dibs yet?" I can tell the little hamster wheel in Miles' head is turning.

"We've met. Let's just leave it at that and grab something to drink." I nudge him along, and Marino brings up the rear.

Bottles of soda in hand, Frick and Frack pick the ideal spot to sit, just like I expected them to. Far enough away to maintain the appearance of not giving a shit and close enough to make our presence impossible to ignore. I drop into the only chair with a direct sightline to the girls' table.

The conversation, if you can call it that, between Miles and Marino swirls around me, but my eyes are continually drawn to a long chestnut braid and golden, tanned skin. Her friend keeps flicking eye-daggers in my direction, but it doesn't deter me in the slightest.

Something about Blue Eyes is as intriguing as it is annoying.

Younger than me, I'd peg her around nineteen. She's gorgeous, sure, but my world has no shortage of hot women. This one, though, gives off a bizarre, vicious-meets-vulnerable vibe that makes my skin hum and my chest tighten. Her performance in the coffee shop and how she clapped back at me in her cabin makes me want to push her further to see if she breaks, and I have no idea why.

One more overblown laugh from this direction has her turning around and confronting us with a sexy, smartass smirk. When she kisses the tips of her middle fingers and flips us off with both hands, I swallow my appreciative chuckle and continue to glare. Miles slaps a hand comically over his heart, and Marino laughs like a buffoon, while I force myself to keep my expression dark. When she finally breaks eye contact, disappointment echoes through me.

Fuck, what the hell are you thinking? Remember the look she gave you earlier? She's nothing special—just another rando looking to bag a rock star. I need to teach her a lesson and flush her out of my system.

Apparently, the girls have had enough of our shit, and the two of them stalk out of the cafeteria. I count to thirty in my head before giving the guys a lame excuse about being tired from my flight and following suit.

When I shove through the back doors into the chill

night air, she's standing on the path alone. Staring out toward the blackness of the Sound, she doesn't move as the door clicks softly shut behind me. Her friend appears to have abandoned her, giving me the perfect opportunity.

My footsteps fall silently as I close the short distance between us.

All right, Blue Eyes, time to show you who's boss.

CHAPTER EIGHT

Hali

"Hey, gimme two minutes?" Vann asks, already backing away toward the washroom at the end of the hall. "I have to pee like crazy, and I don't want to have to find a bush on the way back. I'll be quick, I promise."

"Sure, whatever. I'll wait outside for you." My need to be as far away as possible from the cafeteria is overwhelming.

The sun has long dipped below the horizon, and full darkness has nearly swallowed the dusk. Evenly spaced knee-high lights illuminate the wide main pathway, as well as the smaller ones snaking off toward each cabin. Engulfed by the quiet, my shoulders involuntarily tense with dread.

Back in Folkestone, even the deepest silence screamed, and I grew used to being permanently on edge. Dark thoughts always poison every bit of light I manage to find until all that's left is cruelty and crushing loneliness. My father made sure of that.

But this time nothing happens. Instead, the faint scent of fresh pine riding the cool breeze acts like a balm, soothing nerves worn raw by fear and pain. With each breath, my tension fades a little more. Caught up in the unusual calm this place is weaving around me, I don't register I have company until he speaks.

"Shouldn't be out here alone at night." His grit-wrapped silken voice is pitched low, but it still makes me jump. My momentary complacency disadvantaged me, and I'm guessing Ty took somehow knew to take full advantage of it.

He moves to stand directly in front of me before taking a deliberate step forward. His proximity forces me to take one back in response. We do this dance a handful of times, neither of us saying a word. Reason tells me I should be afraid; this stranger is quite literally backing me into a corner. Fear isn't my primary emotion, though. For some messed up reason, the electric tingle racing over my skin comes from an altogether different, though equally primal, one. One that makes my thighs clench.

My back meets the cold stone of the rear wall, and he takes a final step forward, reducing what was a small gap between us to nothing. The heat radiating through each point of contact between his body and mine sends my senses into a tailspin. His pulse is visible in the hollow of his throat, the flutter mirroring the spike in my own heart rate. The seductive scent of his skin makes me want to lick his neck, and I bite the tip of my tongue to curb the urge.

Ty's an asshole, but I can't deny he's also insanely hot. I'm sure he goes through women like toilet paper—use them, throw them out, on to the next. So, maybe a dose of his own medicine will help deflate his rock star ego. As a bonus, driving him crazy might make being stuck in this place a little more entertaining.

Shadowed and discreet, this small nook formed by the angles of the lodge's architecture is intimate and perfect for a quickie hookup. The anticipation of the pressure of his lips has mine parting slightly, and my breathing turns shallow and quick.

He walks his fingertips up my arm from wrist to shoulder, the warmth of his touch penetrating the thin material of my hoodie. My responding shiver curves his mouth into a smug, knowing smirk.

Abruptly, the same hand moves to encircle my throat, pinning me against the wall. His grip raises my chin, forcing my eyes to his. I recognize this display of dominance, the threat of him suddenly squeezing tight enough to cut off my airflow ever-present. He leans in closer, his breath soft against my ear.

"You owe me an Americano."

My body goes rigid and my skin flushes with instant recognition.

The asshole who cut the line at the coffee shop.

"Not so big and bad now, are you, Rich Girl?" he purrs, both seductive and threatening. I refuse to let him have the upper hand though, so I meet his glare without flinching and raise a single, manicured eyebrow in challenge.

Ty tightens his grip around my throat slightly. The increased pressure shifts the balance between shock and sexual desire even more heavily in desire's favor. The perversity of it floods me with a dusky laugh. Either the sound itself or the sensation of the soft skin of my throat moving against his rough palm appears to shift his original intent. Instead of the sharp, cold stare meant to instill fear, a spark of lust flares in his stormy eyes. His smirk falters, becoming less asshole bravado and more fascinated curiosity. At the same time, his cock hardens where it's pressed against my hip through his jeans.

Oh no, you're not getting off that easily.

"I'm still big and bad, dickhead," I sneer. "You're gonna have to do better than that if you want to steal my crown." My crimson lips part, baring perfect white teeth in a cruel smile. I drive my knee sharply into his groin, forcing a grunt of pain from him. His grip on me loosens, and I slip from his grasp just as Vann appears on the steps.

The palm so recently around my throat is now firmly

planted on the wall in front of him as he tries to breathe away his bruised nuts. To add an extra sprinkle of insult to his injury, I reach out and pinch his tight ass on my way past before I break into a jog to meet up with my roommate. His deep, albeit somewhat wheezy, growl follows me, telling me I may have won this round but that our game is far from over.

the bright
lightly swirls

Ty

God, I'd kill for a beer right now.

Stripped to my boxers, the leather of the recliner in my small living room is cold against my skin. I sit, legs splayed, to allow my mistreated boys some room to breathe. The anger and adrenaline pumping through my veins tighten my jaw.

How the fuck does she keep getting the upper hand? Just when I think I'm in control of the situation, she flips the script, and I end up with a flattened ego or a bruised nutsack.

It took a good five minutes to stand up straight and another five for me to shuffle my sorry ass back here. Dropping my head against the back of the chair, I close my eyes and let the remnants of pain fuel a few outrageous revenge fantasies. The fucked up thing is that while they all start with me destroying her in some very

public forum, they all end with her being completely naked.

I swear my boxers just shrank three sizes, so I reach a hand down to shift things around. Instead, I find myself lowering them enough to allow my rigid cock to spring free. The accompanying tightening of my balls as the cool cabin air caresses them is an exquisite pain.

Gripping my shaft, I imagine how good it would be to punish that smart-ass mouth, to thrust deep and hard between her luscious red lips as she sucked me off. I'd shoot my load down her throat, making sure she swallowed every drop, before returning the favor, spreading her wide and licking her clit until she came in a writhing, shivering rush. The thought of sliding my tongue through her wetness shoves me over the edge, and I come hard enough to make me moan out loud in the darkened silence of the cabin.

Spent and sticky and sore, I grit my teeth in frustration.

Damn it, damn it, damn it. How did that go from me face-fucking her in punishment to eating her out in worship? Even in my fantasies, she's coming out on top. I need to nip this shit in the bud.

CHAPTER TEN

Hali

A delicious scent permeates the mantle of sleep, and I wake up to Vann's empty and neatly made bed across the room. What sounds like a television weather report filters in from the living room, warning of cloudy skies and the potential for rain.

Sounds like a great day to stay under the covers.

My little blanket cocoon is cozy and warm, so I squeeze my eyes shut again. Snuggling down, I do my best to ignore the fantastic smell and the memory of Ty's voice.

Once Vann's breathing grew even with sleep last night, curiosity got the better of me. I quietly pulled my laptop from the nightstand drawer and tiptoed out to the living room. Perched on the edge of the couch, earbuds in, I chastised myself multiple times before finally caving and opening a browser window.

What I expected to be a confirmation of Ty's douchebag ways, turned into something completely *un*expected.

I wanted him to be a shitty musician, a shitty friend, a shitty human. Sprinkled among the standard rock star antics, what I found were quotes from other artists raving about how great he was to work with. A blog post interviewing somebody named Ryan Kessworth, talking about how they'd been best friends since childhood. Candid photos of the band at various charity events, and silly selfies with fans.

Damn it. Okay, so maybe he's not a total jackass. But he can't be a nice guy, sexy as hell, and talented, right?

Wrong.

Navigating to YouTube, I spent the better part of an hour watching fan-recorded videos with millions of hits of Heroin Heartbreak playing live, and interview clips from various media outlets. Then I stumbled on a video date stamped a year ago, posted by somebody calling themselves RockSteady.

Ty, alone, seated on the edge of what appeared to be an empty stage, elegant fingers plucking the strings of a white acoustic guitar. Dressed in ripped jeans and a plain, black T-shirt, his thick, dark hair in disarray, he was beautiful. When he raised his head, eyes closed, and began to sing softly, my throat tightened. I wasn't even listening to the words. The stark emotion painted across his features, and the pain in the rasp of his smoky voice was what touched something inside me. Some long-hidden remnant of the girl I lost years ago and the woman I so badly wanted to be.

Instinct whispered to me that, at that moment, he had no idea he was being recorded. The vulnerability, the longing, the *ache* that he expressed was too private, too raw.

Chiding myself for being a sap, I swiped at the tears beading my lashes and snapped the laptop closed. Back in bed, my computer tossed haphazardly on the nightstand, I pulled the covers up and fell into a deep, dreamless sleep.

In the light of day, I wonder if I imagined what spoke to me in that video last night. I'd be lying if I didn't admit to my secret self that part of me hopes it was all real.

"Breakfast is ready," my far too chipper bunkmate singsongs, breaking my reverie. She sets something down with a thunk on the nightstand beside me and jostles the edge of the bed as she sits down. My stomach rumbles in appreciation at the rich aroma filling the air.

Unable to resist any longer, I yawn, stretch, and open my eyes. Spying the gooey goodness on the blue stoneware plate beside me, I tear off a piece of the still-warm dough. As soon as the spicy-sweet flavor hits my tastebuds, I groan with pleasure.

"Cinnamon buns? Did you make these?" I lick the sticky icing from my fingertips, allowing myself to savor every bit. "They're incredible." Chewing muffles my words, but she gets the gist.

"I was up early." She shrugs. "When I can't sleep, I bake. Some of my insomnia bouts could have fed small towns." Her tone is even and matter-of-fact, but something dark and sad shimmers in her eyes, dimming her light. She quickly changes the subject, and the shadow slips away, leaving bubbly, energetic Vann in its wake. "Don't forget we're going shopping this afternoon." She stands and bounces to the doorway. "Group starts in an hour. I'll wait for you in the kitchen so we can walk up together."

Group therapy. A required component of the program here and something that appeals to me about as much as flat-ironing my tongue. The thought of peeling open old wounds to be judged by a bunch of randos makes my stomach churn, forcing me to set the remainder of the sticky pastry back on the plate.

Concern about the cloud that settled briefly over Vann gives me something to focus on besides my own fears. It was vaguely familiar, a shiver I almost recognized. But it's not my place to ask, as much as I might want to.

Stop giving a shit. You're here for one reason, and it's not to make friends.

My conscience reminds me my roommate has been nothing but kind to me, and as far as potential friends go, she's a pretty damn good candidate, but I stifle it.

Reluctantly I throw off the covers and brace my bare feet against the chilly floor. Deciding to forgo a shower, I pull on faded jeans and a soft blue sweater that matches my eyes before shuffling down the hall to the bathroom. A quick face wash, teeth brush, and a swipe of blush, mascara, and gloss, and I'm good to go.

Back in the bedroom, I snag a hair tie from beside the bed and twist my hair up into a messy bun. With my fingers busy securing the ends, my eyes flick to the window next to me and nearly bug out of my head before I leap back out of sight.

Being tired and even more pissed off than usual yesterday, my brain registered the room's windows but ignored what was *outside* them. One faces the main path, curtained by dense trees that afford a significant amount of privacy. But the one along the back wall looks directly into a matching window in the accommodations next to us. The few trees on this side are much sparser and aren't enough to block the sight of my temporary neighbor.

Ty, obviously fresh out of the shower, is naked except for a towel wrapped around his hips and the water beading his lean but well-muscled torso. The voyeur in me is unable to resist the pull of a better look. My glance is drawn to the insane V disappearing under his towel.

Daaammmmmmmmnnnnnnn, he is sexy. The 'I want to lick you all over and find out what you taste like' kind of sexy.

Of course, he picks that moment to raise his head, and my glance flies up to his gorgeous face. The smirk that curves his lips is dirty as hell, and I can guess his next move before he makes it.

Because it's precisely what I would do.

Just as his beringed and tattooed hand moves to drop the towel, I spin away in a violent and awkward mockery of a pirouette. My toes smash into the bed frame with enough force to make me collapse onto my mattress in a hail of f-bombs. Vann comes flying down the hall and slides to a stop courtesy of sock feet on hardwood. If I wasn't busy clutching my foot and yowling, I'd probably be impressed.

"Are you okay? What happened?"

"Mmmm-hmmm, I'm good." The words squeeze themselves out from between gritted teeth. My two smallest toes hurt like hell, but the initial concern that I separated them from their siblings has passed. They're definitely still attached, but it's going to make the walk up to the lodge extra fun. "Saw Sasquatch outside and kicked the bed frame in my hurry to snap a photo."

"What? Where?" Vann shrieks and runs to the side window. I smother my laughter and settle for shaking my head. The morning has taught me two things so far —my bunkmate is gullible as hell, and the boy next door is very, very, naughty and looks even more fuckable half-naked.

I wonder how tasty he looks fully naked?

The thought elicits a dirty grin of my own, and I spend a few seconds savoring it before standing. Gingerly, I put weight on my foot and smooth my top that's gotten all twisted. Inhaling deeply through my nose and letting it out in a whoosh, I steel myself for the incoming group therapy shitstorm.

"Come on, Sasquatch stalker, let's go." The urge to mock her further is strong, but I swallow it. Grabbing the sleeve of her fluffy, red, sweater, I tug her away from the window and out the door.

From the minute I walk in, every fiber of my soul screams at me to turn around and run right back out. Therapy in general makes me cringe, but this goes beyond that. Some sixth sense deep in my gut says this is a particularly bad idea. I choose to ignore it, though, as well as the inane chatter flitting around me. I take a seat in the circle of chairs between Vann and a pale wisp of a girl who looks like she'd crumple in a heavy wind.

When Ty saunters in, he plants himself directly across from me, legs splayed, arms folded behind his head. Despite the shit-eating grin on his face, or maybe because of it, he's sex personified. It's not just his looks, either. He exudes a powerful sensuality and confidence that runs deeper than that, a magnetism that demands your attention as soon as he walks into a room.

Right now, *his* attention is focused on my tits, happily eye-groping them through my form-fitting sweater. While I find his overt attempt to unnerve me amusing, a couple of the other girls in the room look less than pleased. Their jealousy-laden glares are easy for me to dismiss and I'm about to ask Vann who my new fans are when Mari arrives. She strides to the circle's empty seat, and all conversation halts.

"Good morning, everybody. We have two newcomers with us today. Please give them both a big welcome." She beams her smile around the room, making eye contact with each individual, acknowledging their presence as part of the circle. A few voices mumble sullen hellos, but the catty bitches who are still giving me the stink eye don't say a word. And Ty just keeps on smirking at me. Mari continues. "We have a tradition here when new guests join us. Hali, why don't you start and tell us a bit about yourself?"

Like I would ever intentionally share anything real with a roomful of strangers.

She waits for my response and the air thickens with judgment and anticipation. Eleven pairs of eyes stare at me like a sideshow attraction, and for possibly the first time in my life I'm at a loss for words. Tongue-tied by anger, embarrassment, and outright panic, I take the easy way out and fall back on the familiarity of old patterns—shock and awe.

"I'm Hali. Psycho Daddy's dead, Mommy's a dismissive nutjob with murderous tendencies, and I got dumped here because nobody gives a shit if I fall off the face of the earth."

The unmistakable snickers of the Stink Eyes break the shocked silence following my abrupt statement. Mari shuts them up with a warning glance. Vann reaches out and squeezes my forearm gently, her empathetic gesture completely foreign and making me flinch.

"We're happy to have you here, Hali." Mari clears her throat. "Just so you're aware, a few simple rules apply to all of our group sessions. First and forem—" She's interrupted by an older woman appearing in the doorway, breathless and flushed.

"I'm sorry, Mari, but Miss Hunter has gone and locked herself in the bathroom again. She's demanding to speak to you before she'll come out." The woman is sheepishly apologetic and wringing her hands.

Mari turns back to address the circle. "Hang tight for a few minutes, everybody. I'll be right back."

She follows the other woman from the room, leaving us to our own devices.

Of all the things I am, highly observant is not the least of them. Being the target of my father's often unpredictable psychotic rage and abuse, I was forced to learn to read a room faster and better than most. While the majority of the group appears distracted by their own personal demons, picking their nails, biting their lips, and refusing to make eye contact, there are a few notable exceptions.

Vann has started exuding waves of anxiety, like a radio tuned to a station filled with nothing but static. Her gaze darts around the room like prey and I swear she's vibrating. I'd bet money that if she could crawl under her chair and hide, she would.

Ty is still Ty, and an asshole level of cocky confidence radiates from his lounging form. Although, something about the set of his jaw and the way he keeps twisting one of his rings makes me wonder how much of his nonchalance is contrived.

Then there's the Stink Eye bitches beside him. One blonde, one flaming red. Like coiled snakes ready to strike, they hold themselves still and taut, the redhead flicking her tongue out every so often to lick her bottom lip.

Those two are going to be a problem.

If the daggers they keep staring at me are any indication, they're aiming straight for me, and I refuse to be an easy target. Self-preservation mode kicks in, and the cold, callous, worst possible version of myself slips into place, ready to deflect any barbs they sling my way. Usually, it fits like a glove, molded perfectly to every damaged and cracked bit of my psyche. Today, it fits more like a cheap suit made of shitty material and baggy in all the wrong places.

Venom spikes the air as they open their mouths, and

I hate them for forcing me to be exactly what everybody back in Folkestone thinks I am.

Vicious and cruel.

From the outside, I doubt I look any different than I did thirty seconds ago, but every one of my muscles is rigid with tension. I'm ready for them to come at me with their barrage of bullshit.

"Awwwww, look. Poor little Vannessa is about to piss her pants. What's the matter, stepdaddy fucker?" the blonde spits at my bunkmate, who appears to be trying her damnedest to will herself to vanish into thin air.

Wait, what? They're going after kind, bubbly, doesn't-seem-likely-to-hurt-a-fly Vann?

"Scared we might tell your new roomie how messed up you really are?" The redhead asks before turning to me, all doe-eyes and fluttering lash extensions. "Don't let her little innocent act fool you; she's anything but." She snickers, a cold, callous sound. "Vannessa's stepdaddy comes into her bedroom at night and plays with her dirty pussy until she's all wet and begging for it. Then he fucks her silly. That's why her mom hates her so much." She makes a tsk tsk sound when tears start to slip down Vann's cheeks. "She tells everybody he forces her, but we all know the truth. She likes what he does to her. She begs for it."

Blondie elbows Red conspiratorially, and they both start laughing, a harsh, dry sound typical of mean girls everywhere. The kind of laugh meant to belittle and degrade, devoid of humanity or common decency. Ty sits silently, his face the picture of disgusted disbelief as the two douchebags congratulate themselves on their cruelty. His buddies from the other night start making lewd faces in Vann's direction. I look around the circle, waiting for somebody to speak in my roommate's defense but everybody else is either laughing or busy examining non-existent lint on their sweaters.

"Why don't you shut the fuck up?" My words surprise everybody in the room, myself included. I'm used to playing offense—hell, I've practically made it my job to make people cry. But witnessing Vann's overwhelming non-verbal distress has me switching to defense. Plus, even in the incredibly short time I've known her, I'm confident that every one of the claims they're making against her is false.

"Nobody asked for your opinion, bitch," Redhead sneers, turning her vitriol in my direction.

"Never fucking stopped me before, *bitch*. Leave her alone."

"You got something to say on the subject, stand up and say it." Red and Blondie both uncoil from their folding metal chairs and take a few menacing steps toward me, intent on physically threatening me into backing down. Little do they know they're up against the MVP of mean girls. These two aggressively posturing idiots aren't even in the same ballpark. In one heartbeat, I'm on my feet, in their faces in another.

"You want to come after me, bring it. But if you don't leave Vann alone, I have enough pent-up rage and moral ambiguity to end you two twats without hesitation. Sit. The fuck. Down."

"Everybody, sit down. Now!" Mari marches to her seat and sweeps us all with a disapproving glare. "Who's going to explain what just happened here?"

Crickets.

"Okay, we'll play it your way. Hali, you're confined to your cabin until we can discuss the ramifications of threatening other guests and what The Overlook's zero-tolerance policy on bullying means. Vann, please go with her."

Damn it. This is what happens when you stick your neck out to help somebody. You end up getting shafted.

My roommate and I stand together, and we couldn't be more different—me, head held high, and her with her shoulders slumped and eyes glued to the floor. Ty mutters something unintelligible behind us, and the sound of his voice is a match to kerosene. My hand on Vann's arm halts her, and I spin to face the guy who's been nothing but a pain in my ass since the first time we crossed paths.

"You enjoy being a dick, McInnis? I find it hard to believe that your life is so perfect that you're entitled to have an opinion about anybody else's." As the words leave my lips, their rampant hypocrisy isn't lost on me. Neither is the brief glimpse of pain that flares into anger behind his eyes before he smothers it with a smug grin. "Keep it up, Ty. Payback's a bitch."

"Oh, don't worry, I've got no problem keeping it up." He winks at me.

"Ty, enough." Mari looks like her head might pop right off; her hippie chill evaporated. "Hali, Vann, back to your cabin. Now."

Shooting a last death glare at Ty, I stalk haughtily out of the room. But that fleeting look in his eyes lingers in the back of my mind like the echo of a song you can't quite remember the words to.

CHAPTER ELEVEN

Ty

After Hali and Vann leave the room, Mari quickly dismisses the group and makes her own exit. If I was smart, I'd just go back to my cabin and stay the hell out of it, but somebody losing their spot here because of Erissa and Sabrina is too much bullshit for me to choke down.

"Can I help you, dear?" The older woman from earlier is back behind her desk in the lodge entryway.

"I'm good, thanks. Just looking for Mari."

"She should be back shortly. Been a busy morning around here." She tut-tuts at me and shakes her head.

"Not a problem. I'll grab a seat." I lower myself into one of the large leather armchairs in front of the flag-stone fireplace.

My fingers drum a slow rhythm on the side of the chair while I stare out through the large picture window, going over everything that happened this morning in my head.

Very little surprises me when it comes to women anymore. My career has afforded me access and opportunity beyond even the wildest teenage wet dream. Each experience had compounded one universal truth—latex miniskirts, leather pants, or plain cotton T-shirts, it's all the same when it ends up on the floor at my feet. Peel back those layers, and they all want to use me or be used by me. Mothers, daughters, sisters...the only difference is age and experience.

So, what the hell is it about this one that's so different?

She's all swagger and sharp edges and carefully crafted mean, but intuition tells me she has more depth under all of that than anybody I've ever met. Like a feral cat, she'll claw your eyes out to make a point, but she harbors something soft and scared inside, longing for a respite from all the noise.

Her very existence—and my reaction to it—makes me nuts. I'm pissed off, intrigued, and horny all at once.

Even before the shitshow in group this morning, she had me in knots.

Sleep was an elusive bitch last night, finally making an appearance only as the first hint of dawn touched the window next to my bed. Three hours later, I dragged my ass out of bed and showered, hoping to wash some of the cranky and tired away.

When that didn't work, I gave my hair a quick towel dry and wrapped the plush bath sheet around my hips.

Back in the cabin's single bedroom, movement in the residence next to mine drew my attention.

With her arms above her head, the shirt she was wearing hiked up just enough to expose a sliver of smooth, tanned midriff. The jolt that charged through me at that little slice of skin went straight to my dick, and I glanced down to find it straining enthusiastically against the towel.

Even now, just thinking about how she looked pumps a flood of adrenaline through my veins, forcing me to my feet.

What the fuck is wrong with me? I have access to more pussy than I know what to do with, but I'm pitching tents over a glimpse of my neighbor's belly button?

But it's not that simple, and that's what scares me the most. Her beauty and her broken speak to me in equal measure. As much as I hunger for the taste of her lips, I want to *know* her—the mundane and the monumental. What makes her smile. How she likes her eggs. Who left their dirty fingerprints all over her soul.

And I can't go there, can't let myself even entertain the idea of the kind of vulnerability truly knowing her would require.

The last time I let a woman in, it almost killed me.

My resolve to set the record straight about what

happened in group starts to waver the more I pace. If I keep my mouth shut, Hali will be gone. Problem solved.

Except that's not my style.

A door slams closed down the hall and makes my decision for me. Footsteps stride toward the back of the lodge, and I catch sight of long blonde hair.

"Mari," I call, following her.

"Ty." She flashes a quick, tight smile over her shoulder at me, but doesn't stop. "Can we talk later? I need to deal with what happened in group." She's about to push through the back doors when I grasp her forearm, halting her.

"About that, I think you might be missing a few pertinent details. I respect your zero-tolerance policy for bullying and bullshit, but you don't know the whole story."

"What details? Seems pretty cut and dried to me. Hali was out of control." She grimaces and shakes her head. "Damn it. I can't talk to you about this. When you're here, you're a client, not a friend."

"Look, they went after Vann. Hard. Honestly, if that happened to somebody I considered a friend, I would have thrown down, too. They were vulgar. Hali was only defending somebody who wouldn't, or couldn't, defend themselves."

And just like she seemed surprised at defending her roommate, here I am defending her.

"Are you sure you don't have some kind of ulterior

motive in mind? Like the longer she sticks around, the better your chances are of getting into her pants?"

She might as well have punched me in the face. Her words leave me stunned and speechless for a few seconds while I process what just came out of her mouth.

"Jesus H., Mari. Seriously? I thought you knew me better than that." My vision darkens, clouded by anger and hurt. "Even if I was that much of a prick, why would I fuck around with some cranky teenage headcase? The last thing I need is another fucking clinger." Emotion gets the better of me, and as the words leave my lips, I regret them. I shove past her and out the doors, turning back briefly on the top step. "Do what you want. The other two were in the wrong, not her. When you're done reading her the riot act, go fuck yourself."

She swears under her breath and calls after me as I stride away, but I choose to ignore her.

Back in my cabin, the barren kitchen cupboards mock me as I slam through them and seethe. Ever since I ran into Hali at the coffee shop, she's been nothing but a distraction.

What do I care if her rich, entitled ass gets turfed from the program? She can go back to fucking frat boys in their expensive cars and drown in her drug habit or whatever the hell got her thrown in here. I'm done. No more trying to fix situations that have shit all to do with me. Every man for himself.

Anger quickly shifts to raging frustration because the thought of her in the backseat, sweaty and panting, skirt shoved up and legs spread wide, has my traitorous dick standing at attention again. The granite counter is cold under my fist as I hammer on it multiple times, trying to dim the vision of her in my head. Sucking in a harsh gulp of air, I count to five and wonder for the zillionth time in the past day what the fuck is wrong with me.

My guts growl, and I realize I haven't had a single thing to eat yet today. A glance at my phone says the shuttle to town isn't leaving for another hour. Unless I want to go back up to the main lodge—which I don't— I'm screwed for food. So, I pretend the gnawing in the pit of my stomach is nothing more than hunger pangs, flop down on my bed, and do my best to forget the girl next door.

CHAPTER TWELVE

Hali

Our walk back is heavy with unspoken emotion. The crunch of gravel underfoot punctuates Vann's embarrassment and the pain of what just happened with every step.

As soon as we're inside the cabin, she beelines for the bathroom. The door lock clicks behind her, followed by the familiar sound of water rushing full blast into the sink.

Oh, Vann, I feel you, girl. I really do.

The messed-up thing is, I recognize it from both sides, the aggressor and the victim. And I have no idea how to deal with that.

I trade my sweater for a long, black V-neck shirt. Lost in my head, I perch dejectedly on the small living room couch to await the arrival of my executioner. After

seeing how pissed Mari was, dollars to donuts today is my last day at The Overlook.

The funny thing is, if somebody had mentioned this place to me six months ago, I would've laughed in their face, tossed my hair, and flounced away. Probably after grinding their ego to dust under the heel of my favorite red-soled stilettos. That version of me wouldn't give a rat's ass about getting kicked out because I'd never have agreed to come here in the first place.

Something changed when my father died, though. Like a door that had been locked forever suddenly opened. Just a crack, but enough to let a sliver of light start to push back the darkness I'd been born into.

Yeah, sure, I was a bitch about it. I couldn't let my mother think it would be easy to disappear me from her shiny new lease on life. She didn't deserve that. But maybe, for the first time, I believed *I* deserved something more than the atrocities and abuse shoved down my throat.

One thing Eleanor said stuck with me, though I'll choke myself out before admitting it to anybody. The Overlook was a chance for me to find my own path. To be who I want to be rather than the beat-up bag of lip gloss and malevolence my father made me. To have that chance shot to shit in less than thirty-six hours bothers me. And the fact that it bothers me as much as it does, bothers me that much more.

Now I have two choices. On the one hand, I can

maintain the status quo. Go back to Folkestone and continue being the nasty, never-quite-good-enough, self-loathing, havoc-wreaking bitch everybody hates. Easy as pie. But before I screwed it up right out of the gate, I was cautiously excited about what the *other* hand had to offer. For all my bluster and bullshit, the idea of a fresh start held intense appeal.

If I had kept my stupid mouth shut, I wouldn't be in this mess. Vann's a big girl. She can take care of herself.

Except that isn't true. Everything that went down makes me damn near positive she's been a target of those shitty girls, or girls like them, before. They went straight for the jugular as soon as Mari left the room and knew what buttons to push to inflict maximum damage.

You should've stayed out of it, you idiot. Look where it got you. Why try to save somebody when nobody's ever tried to save you?

My reaction to my roommate's palpable fear and discomfort flipped the script on me for the first time. The burn of red-hot rage in tandem with the urge to protect anybody other than myself was new to me. And if I'm being frank, I have no idea where it came from.

A firm knock interrupts my runaway train of thought. My breath coming shallow and fast, forcing myself to cross to the cabin door and open is one of the hardest things I've ever done.

I wonder if this is what walking the plank is like.

The image of myself in an old-timey dress, bodice

torn, inching my way along a wooden board high above an angry sea makes me giggle. Add in a one-eyed pirate captain, and the giggle turns hysterical. An uncomfortable, high-pitched sound. It abruptly cuts off when I remember no swashbuckling hero will swoop in to save me in this story.

"Hi, Hali. Can we talk?"

Rather than answer, I simply step aside to let Mari pass. She turns to face me, and a sickening wave of panic compels me to speak first. I shouldn't care what this woman thinks of me, but I can't help it. The thought of her telling me I'm a horrible individual not worthy of redemption or kindness makes me want to throw up. My only option is to make it look like leaving is my idea instead of hers. Maybe then I can force myself to believe it, too.

"Look, therapy isn't for me, and this isn't working, so I'm just going to pack my shit and call an Uber or something. I'll figure out a flight at the airport." The words tumble out of my mouth, tripping over each other in my haste to get them out. "For the record, I didn't wake up with the intent to threaten anybody, which is actually new for me. But even though those girls only said three sentences to Vann, each one was more horrible than the last." My feet are itching to be moving, shuffling closer to the bedroom with each breath. "My mother should have known better. I'm my father's daughter, and people like me can't be fixed. Sorry for wasting your time."

The air is getting thinner, and I can't draw a deep breath. It's like I'm trying to suck oxygen into my shoulders instead of my lungs—high, tight, and wholly distressing. Prickles of sweat, hot and cold at the same time, break out all over my body, dampening the skin under my breasts and the small of my back. An intense wave of nausea floods my mouth with saliva and my vision tunnels.

Mari steps to me and grips my upper arms just as everything tilts about three inches to the left. If she wasn't holding on to me, I'd be on my ass.

What the hell is happening to me? I can't breathe. I can't see. Am I dying? If this is what dying is like, I'll pass, thanks. Zero stars. Do not recommend.

The prospect of kicking the bucket before I've even had a chance to find out what's *in* the bucket does nothing except freak me out more. My chest becomes an unbearably tight drum, my heart pounding out a frantic beat. A small squeak that might be either laughter or terror escapes me. Nausea swells again, forcing me to clamp my lips shut to avoid puking all over Mari's pretty sweater.

"Hali, listen to me. Focus on my face. Take a deep breath in through your nose and let it out slowly through your mouth." She adopts a controlled breathing pattern, but I keep shaking my head as my heart pounds triple-time, trying to push blood to extremities that are turning ice cold. "Like me, Hali. Do it just like me." She's nothing if not persistent, and I start to mimic her breaths, haltingly at first but slowly finding the rhythm. "You're having a panic attack. You're safe, you're not dying, and it'll pass."

Turns out she's right. A few minutes pass, and my knees unlock, allowing her to guide me to the couch. Another few, and I can speak coherently, though quietly. My heart is still pounding, and adrenaline makes my hands shake.

"Well, that was embarrassing."

"No need to be embarrassed. It happens." She shrugs, her tone reassuring.

"Give me a sec, and I'll pack my stuff and get out of your hair."

"Obviously, since you're not an *inmate*," she winks, "you're free to leave anytime, but I'd rather you didn't."

"What? You want me to stay?" My brows draw together, and she nods.

"I do."

"After the scene this morning, I figured I was out."

"Hali, if I had to ask somebody to leave every time we had an outburst in group, there'd never be anyone here." She sits down beside me. "You deserve complete transparency, though. That was outside the usual conflict, and based on what I witnessed, I would have been obligated to remove you from the program for bullying." We make eye contact, and I can tell she's one hundred percent serious. "Ty stopped me on my way down here and explained what really happened."

"I'm sorry, who did what now?"

"While threatening other guests is forbidden and can never happen again." She pauses to flash me a stern expression. "I know you were sticking up for Vann."

The relief that courses through me warms my chilly feet and relaxes my shoulders, temporarily overshadowing my shock at Ty defending me.

"They were so awful." My voice is quiet, and I cringe inwardly, aware of how many times I've sounded just like them.

"Unfortunately, I didn't hear what they said, only your response. I don't have any grounds to remove them at this point as anything that happened before I arrived would be seen as hearsay. But I will be monitoring them going forward." She pauses. "Can I ask you something? What was it like, defending Vann?"

My reputation obviously precedes me, so I don't blame her for asking.

"Unexpected." Where my usual response would be snide and bitchy, I choose to take a baby step toward the 'different path' idea. "Vann's business is her own, and it shouldn't be up for public discussion." I shrug and stare down at my fingers twisting knots around each other in my lap. "Thank you for letting me stay." Her kindness has me floundering—I'm so unfamiliar with anybody extending it my way.

"Vann, are you okay?" Mari stands, moving to the still pale but far steadier girl as she appears in the doorway.

"Can we not talk about it right now, please?"

Mari looks like she wants to insist, but Vann's pleading expression appears to change her mind, and she nods.

"We'll schedule a one-on-one with your therapist, and you can discuss it then." She checks the time. "The shuttle leaves in fifteen minutes. Let's go, ladies or poor Hali's going to have to live on muffins and potato chips until the next trip to town."

Poor Hali. Not once in my entire life has anybody ever used those two words together in a sentence.

The thought brings a tiny smile to my lips. Picturing the looks on the faces of those two bitches when they realize I'm staying makes it even bigger. Vann nudges me, a look of unspoken thanks on her pretty features and we grab our jackets and follow Mari up to the main lodge.

CHAPTER THIRTEEN

Hali

As I understand it, the twice-weekly shuttle rides into town for supplies aren't mandatory, and not everybody goes each time. Part of me prays that the girls from this morning decided to forgo this trip. If they start mouthing off, I'm not sure I'll be able to stop myself from choosing violence, and I doubt Mari will look the other way again. When the large SUV comes into view, it's apparent my prayers fell on deaf ears, and the resulting groan comes all the way from my toes.

Ty's lounging against the side of the white vehicle, next to the open rear passenger door. He has an adoring audience of two, the blonde and the redhead from earlier. When the sound of our footsteps alerts them to our presence, all three pause mid-conversation. Ty's gaze is guarded and dismissive, which is both puzzling and annoying given that he defended me, but the other two? If they had their way, Vann and I would burst into flames on the spot.

I swear Mari mutters a few curses under her breath when we approach. But when I turn to look at her in surprise, she's wearing a standard-issue vanilla-bland smile that doesn't quite make it all the way to her eyes.

Vann tenses beside me, her steps slowing as tiny beads of sweat break out along her hairline. Her visible reaction is like a punch to the gut, making me wonder how many people back home have the same response when they see me coming.

Shame flushes my face with heat. Shoving it aside, I try to focus on the outing ahead.

The rock star, the groupies, the basket case, and the bitch. Isn't this going to be fun?

Ty disentangles himself from his female admirers and moves to intercept me like he has something to say. His intense gaze sets off a kaleidoscope of butterflies in my stomach. Before he can speak, a protective instinct screams within me to shut him down. My lips curve into a sultry smirk as I step close enough to whisper in his ear.

"Don't go thinking what you did this morning earns you any points, McInnis. You're still an egotistical dick, and I still wear the crown." Letting my lips graze his earlobe, I reach between us, the movement hidden by the angle of our bodies, and give his junk a squeeze through his jeans. When I clench my hand, his sharp intake of breath sends a shiver racing down my spine. I saunter away with a chuckle, making sure to press my tits against his arm as I brush by and climb into the back of the waiting vehicle. Vann joins me, and Mari sits in the front with the driver, leaving the middle for the other three.

Once on the highway, it takes precisely forty-seven seconds for me to regret the seating arrangements. I'd rather strap myself to the fucking roof than be forced to witness the show in front of us. It may only be a twenty-minute ride, but that's eighteen and a half minutes of adoring groupie bullshit and over-inflated rock star ego too long.

To stop myself from ripping open the door and flinging myself from the moving vehicle, I entertain Vann by pulling ridiculously mocking faces behind their backs. Every time she snickers, one of the girls snaps her head around to glare at us. I give whichever twit it happens to be a big shit-eating grin until she returns to petting Ty.

It's infuriating and gross, the way he's making a show of letting those skanky cows drape all over him. Any self-respecting human wouldn't go near them after the stunt they pulled this morning. I finally turn my face to the window and stare stonily at the landscape flashing by.

When the longest ride in history is finally over, Mari

tells us we have an hour to shop. But what I want more than anything right now is a minute to myself.

"Vann, I need to stretch my legs. I'll meet you inside, okay?"

Before she can respond, I zip up my jacket, jam my hands in the pockets, and take off across the street. The wind lashes my cheeks and lifts the ends of my hair in a chaotic dance. It's colder here in town, and my choice of outwear offers little warmth. My shivers are only partly temperature-related, though. The rest are generated by stormy gray eyes and a certainty that I don't deserve to be here.

The Overlook might be the opportunity I've been waiting for. The first step toward shedding the heavy cloak of my father's sins and stepping out of the darkness he tried so hard to drown me in.

But three certainties sit like lead weights on my chest when I remember how Erissa and Sabrina treated my new roommate.

I know those two are bush league. Amateurs parading around clothed in designer jeans and bad attitudes.

I know I'm the real deal, and the things I've done make their antics pale in comparison.

And I know I don't deserve the second chance I ache so badly for, or the way my pulse picks up every time Ty looks at me.

Inhaling a deep pull of crisp air, I let the chill burn

down into my lungs. Tears hang heavily in my lower lashes, and I swipe a finger under each eye to catch them before they fall.

Suck it up, Torsten.

With my father's declarations of being unlovable and inherently bad ringing in my ears, I turn back toward the market, eyeing it with a mixture of curiosity and distaste.

I shop for high-end clothing and expensive shoes, not food. Getting groceries is an odious task that has always been handled by our housekeeper. Still, I can't put it off any longer. The automatic entrance doors swoosh closed behind me, and I go on a hunt for Vann to plead my case for a shopping buddy.

Out of nowhere, I'm herded from behind into an aisle filled with baking supplies. I'm about to scream my bloody murder when a large, strong, palm clamps tightly over my mouth. His lean body is warm and solid against my back and I recognize the scent of his skin from our last encounter. Without removing his hand, he frog-marches me closer to the shelves in front of us, like we're both looking for something specific housed on them.

"That little stunt you pulled earlier wasn't very nice," Ty murmurs against my ear, the timbre of his voice enough to send an annoying wave of goosebumps dancing over my skin.

Slowly sliding his hand from my lips, he trails the

backs of his knuckles down the side of my neck before squeezing my shoulder. At the same time, his other hand clamps vise-like on my upper arm. To anybody walking by, we appear to be nothing more interesting than a young couple shopping very intently for flour and sugar.

"What do you want, Ty? Didn't get enough ego-stroking on the ride over? Because you're barking up the wrong tree for that kind of shit. I don't stroke any ego except my own." My voice is quiet, but the snark is loud and clear. Hopefully, it masks the unfamiliar emotion twisting up my insides at the thought of those girls throwing themselves at him.

No such luck.

"Jealousy doesn't become you," he purrs against my hair. "Besides, I'm more interested in other kinds of stroking with you." His thumb starts tracing little circles on my shoulder.

"Yeah, like that'll happen," I snort. "I have no interest in stroking your tiny dick, McInnis."

"We've had this discussion. My dick is bigger than you'd know what to do with. You would've seen the proof yourself if you'd kept watching another few seconds this morning." His warm, minty breath fluttering next to my ear is starting to do melty things to my insides. "And who said anything about you doing the stroking?"

Releasing my upper arm, he very deliberately unzips my jacket, letting it fall open. His hand brushes across my nipple and has it standing at attention right through my lacy bra and oversized shirt. Before I can give him any shit, though, he's reaching down and cupping me through my jeans.

"Ty! What the hell?" I'm frozen in place, shocked by his audacity but also more than a little turned on.

"You grabbed mine, so it's only fair I do the same." Except, he doesn't stop there. He pops the button on my jeans with one hand and tugs the zipper down just enough to allow him access. The way his fingers dance teasingly across the sensitive skin of my abdomen under my long T-shirt makes my thighs clench and my breath hitch.

"For fuck's sake, we're in a goddamn grocery store. I may be new to the idea, but I'm pretty sure this isn't what usually happens in one." I try to wriggle out of his grasp, but his grip on my shoulder is iron.

"For fuck's sake, indeed," he says in that smoke-on-silk voice and slips his hand inside my panties.

Frozen in place, I'm powerless as his fingers trace the seam of my pussy lips. My legs threaten to buckle at the contact and the crazy urge to ride his hand right here in the baking aisle is strong.

The sound of an approaching squeaky wheel cuts through my wanton stupor. A white-haired woman who looks to be in her eighties comes around the corner. Her tiny stature is dwarfed by a disproportionately huge shopping cart.

"She's going to see!" My struggles are in vain. All he does is pull me in tighter and make sure my shirt is still covering me to mid-thigh, hiding what his hand is doing.

"Stop flailing, and she won't notice a thing," he whispers with a low burr of laughter.

Anger, nervousness, and white-hot lust war for dominance, but I hold as still as possible and mentally urge the octogenarian to move along. But she doesn't, because that would be too easy.

Just as she comes to a full stop next to us, Ty coats two fingers with my wetness before starting to strum my clit like one of his precious guitars. The added friction from the calluses on his fingertips makes me want nothing more than to spread my legs wider and come all over his hand.

"Excuse me, my dears. I just need one of those bags of powdered sugar in front of you."

"S-s-s-sure," I stammer as she reaches for one, not trusting myself to say anything else. It's taking all of my concentration to choke down my moans and stay upright.

This is the most surreal thing I've ever experienced. I'm being expertly fingered by an actual rock star, who's a good four years older than me, in a small-town grocery store while somebody's grandma is shopping for sugar next to us. How is this even happening?

The woman finally moves on, and I grind my ass into Ty's groin, signaling him to finish what he started.

Only he has other plans.

My release builds, and just as I'm about to come, Ty pulls his hand away and takes a step back, leaving me hanging. It takes me a second to get my legs to stop shaking, but once I do, I turn to face him, confused and more than a little pissed off.

"Uhhh, are you kidding me?"

"I don't kid, Rich Girl. Not about money, music, or pussy, anyway." He bares his teeth in an asshole grin before slipping one of the fingers so recently between my legs into his mouth and tasting it. "Sorry honey, yours just doesn't quite measure up." At that, he saunters away, leaving me unsatisfied and seething.

Goddamn it, who the hell does he think he is? I have a spectacular pussy. I think. Even if I don't, nobody gets away with talking to me that way.

Glancing furtively around, I zip and button my jeans, then take some deep breaths to calm the rage burning in my veins before stomping through the store. I check down each aisle for a glimpse of Vann's long, black hair, while mentally cataloging how many different ways I can separate Ty's junk from the rest of his body. In the second to last row, I spot her at the opposite end, where she's flattened up against shelves stocked with coffee and tea.

What in the actual fuck? Is this the Tinder of grocery stores or something?

The middle-aged man slobbering on her while trying to cop a feel is heavily overweight. His girth dwarfs Vann and jiggles revoltingly in his excitement. Surprisingly agile for a man his size, every time she zigs, he zags.

"Hey, Tiny," I yell. "Get your damn hands off her!" I stride down the aisle toward them. Faced with my wrath, he backs away, palms up, the overhead fluorescents highlighting his severely receding hairline.

"I didn't do nothin' wrong. Them girls told me she missed her daddy so I should show her a little love. They told me she likes to play hard to get, but she didn't mean it." Like a spider to a fly, he turns his attention back to his intended target and reaches one stubby finger under the edge of his too-small shirt. When he digs into his navel looking for lint or buried treasure or whatever the fuck, I gag but force myself to step between him and Vann, baring my teeth in a snarl.

"First, when they try to run, it means they aren't interested, fucktard. Second, oh my fucking ewwwww. Third, who are 'them girls'?" I'm ninety-nine percent positive I already know the answer, but I want to hear him say it.

He's sweating more than an innocent man ever would, beady little eyes flicking left and right as he slowly backs away from the heat of my mocking rage.

What's it like to be prey instead of predator, you disgusting fuck?

My ears pick up the sound of snickering bitches in the next aisle. I grab Vann's arm, tugging her along behind me. Her revolting would-be suitor uses the opportunity to ooze away as quickly as his short, pudgy legs will carry him. I round the aisle's end cap and come face-to-face with my roommate's tormentors.

"Something funny?" My voice is dripping with a warning they choose to ignore.

"Awwww, poor Vannessa. Did you let your next lay slip away?" Both girls jut their bottom lips out in exaggerated pouts.

I take a step forward because this bullshit is going to end right now.

"Problem, ladies?" Mari finds us just in time, the four of us glaring at each other in challenge. Well, okay, three of us glaring, and the fourth half-hidden behind me.

"Nope." I pop the p. "No problem at all."

"Hali and I were just leaving," Vann volunteers and tugs me away, stopping in the coffee aisle to retrieve her half-filled plastic basket.

We finish our shopping in silence, but without further incident, and head back to the SUV. After claiming the middle seats this time and stowing our bags at our feet, she tries to cover her shakiness by rambling about some K-pop band she's obsessed with. I listen with one ear, watching through the tinted window as the two idiots approach, their King Idiot, Ty, hanging back behind them by several steps.

They strut confidently in their five-hundred-dollar boots, swinging their hips and tossing their hair, secure in their positions at the top of the social food chain. It's all too familiar.

The way they tear down anyone they want to, just because they can.

The nasty, entitled attitude that reeks of hidden insecurities.

The ugliness that hides just under their glossy, perfect exteriors.

Every day back in Folkestone, that's what people see when they look at me, only fifty times worse. I just never let myself admit it until now.

No matter what atrocities were visited on me by my father, I'm not a victim—I'm the villain.

CHAPTER FOURTEEN

Hali

During the entire trip back to The Overlook, all I want to do is escape. Vann attempts to engage me in conversation, but I shut down each effort with one-line answers that leave no room for further questions or discussion. Eventually, she stops trying.

The van barely rolls to a stop before I jump out with my bags and scurry down the path to our cabin. This time I'm the one that beelines for the privacy of the bathroom, my groceries, still in the paper bags marked with the store's logo, forgotten on the kitchen table.

On my knees, I puke until dry heaves are all that's left, tears tracking down my cheeks.

Oh God, I'm a terrible person. All of the awful things I've done to people, even to my own half-sister. Was it all because of my father, or is there a part of me that's always been rotten? Are horrible people born or raised?

Back home, so many times I desperately wanted to be anybody but me, to live any life but my own. I never had another option then, but maybe if I wasn't born bad, there's still a chance for me to redeem myself now.

My father was always my keeper. Until this trip, I'd never even traveled without him—no girls' weekends, no school trips. He wouldn't let me out of his sight. And anywhere he took me always involved strange, back-door business dealings. Though he never went as far as actually selling me to the highest bidder, the disgusting men in attendance all undressed me with their eyes, reptilian tongues licking slimy lips in sexual anticipation.

When I complained about their unwelcome stares, he laughed and told me to shut my mouth, that women were only good for two things, and having an opinion wasn't one of them. Then, when the deals went pear-shaped or somebody called him on his bullshit, he blamed me, and I would pay the price for his mistakes.

As long as he was alive, I was trapped. Survival came down to simple math—play the role and the odds of getting my ass kicked, or worse, went from a hundred percent down to about seventy.

The way Vann cowers and shrinks away from Erissa and Sabrina, praying to disappear—that's what *I* do to people, how I make them feel.

Just like my father did to me.

I refuse to look at my reflection while I scrub the

tears from my face and splash cool water against my flushed skin. Taking three big steps backward, I slam the toilet seat lid shut and sit down with a thud while I try to convince myself that I can be better, that I can fix what he left broken.

My racing thoughts are interrupted by a tentative knock.

"Hali? Please talk to me."

So much for the sanctity of a locked shitter.

The exhaustion of trying to make sense of my messed-up life, of being a puppet, of all the hate has wrung me out. Stretching forward, I flick the lock and twist the handle, pushing the door open. Vann stands in the doorway.

"Are you okay?"

"Define 'okay'." I rest my elbows on my knees, cupping my chin in my palms.

"What happened on the ride back? You were fine, and then you weren't. Like somebody flipped a switch."

"Yeah, well, that's me. Ruiner of Lives and Flipper of Switches. I'm not a nice person, Vann, and you're better off staying away from me."

I also apparently have a low-grade vag according to fuckface next door but telling you that would be taking TMI to a whole new level.

"You've been a lot nicer to me than anybody here. Half of them treat me like crap, and the others flat-out ignore me." She slips around the doorframe and slides her back down the wall. Once her butt hits the floor, she pulls her knees to her chest. "Can I tell you something?"

"Sure. Welcome to the Bathroom Confessional. Useful if you need to spill your guts after you spill your guts." My exaggerated wink and attempt at a smile elicit a brief chuckle before she puts her serious face back on.

"Those comments Sabrina and Erissa made in group weren't true."

"Duh. I figured that much. I recognize exactly who those two fuckwits are and all the cunty games they play."

"You do?" She looks surprised.

"I do. Big bank accounts, big egos, big tits, and big chips on their shoulders. This is what I meant about me not being a nice person. I'm one of those girls. Hell, the way I roll, I'm practically their queen." I pinch the bridge of my nose and squeeze my eyes shut against the self-inflicted sting of my words.

"Bullshit."

Hearing her curse is amusing. The fact that she's calling me out makes it even funnier.

"I shit you not. I'm the devil's daughter and have been forced to live up to his morally bankrupt standards my whole life."

She stares at me, all squint-eyed and thoughtful. Almost like she's trying to peer into my soul.

"Nope," she declares with absolute certainty. "Sorry, I don't believe you're a bad person. You wouldn't have stood up for me if you had a black heart. In fact, you wouldn't be here at all, and you sure as heck wouldn't be talking to me like this right now."

The silence stretches between us while she waits for me to say something. Rather than respond, I look up at my reflection in the vanity mirror. Maybe if I stare long enough, I'll see some of what she does.

She takes a deep breath and tries again. "Isn't there some saying about questioning whether you're crazy or not? Like, if you do, you're probably not because a crazy person would never think there was anything to question. Wouldn't it be the same for somebody who was truly bad?"

My brain needs a second to follow her train of thought and process the words, but a tiny glimmer of hope sparks in my chest when it does. I shift my eyes from the mirror to Vann's face and find her staring back at me.

"Do you really think that's true?" The words come out hesitant and soft—two things never associated with me. And that's part of the beauty of being here. Nobody has a clue about the old me. Vann only sees *this* me, the person I'd like the chance to actually be.

"Yes, I do." She speaks with conviction, and her certainty is endearing.

Whatever happens, I hope I leave here with that intact, with at least one person sure I'm not a lost cause.

Because I don't want to be lost anymore.

So, I take the risk and give her the quick and dirty version of my truth.

"My father was sadistic, psychotic, narcissistic—basically, a whole mess of the worst *ics*—heaped onto a raging dumpster fire of evil. The damage he did is unfathomable by anybody who wasn't down in the dark with me."

The words scorch my throat as they spew out, an unstoppable geyser set off by the kindness of a near stranger.

"He broke me and laughed while he did it. Nobody outside our house ever questioned me about the bruises, the scars he left, because he made sure to never mark my skin where they would be visible. But my mother...she was one hundred percent aware and did absolutely nothing." Resentment flares through my melancholy, coloring my words in shades of ash and blood. "Trying to describe his favorite flavors of madness and mayhem, and her contrived ignorance, is like describing the moon to a mouse."

From her spot just inside the doorway, Vann sniffles, eyes leaking, and the corners of her pretty mouth turned down in sadness. I hate that she's wasting her tears on somebody who doesn't deserve them.

"Please don't cry for me. I've done horrible things, terrorized people in ways that make Regina George look like Mary Poppins."

Pins and needles are developing in my legs from

sitting here for so long. I stand and stretch, shaking each leg to get the blood flowing again. Vann pushes herself up from where she's been sitting against the wall and tackle-hugs me.

"I believe in you."

Four words. Not even fancy, twenty-five cent words. But they're worth more than any spoken to me before, punching straight through to my heart. No matter how this ends, I promise myself I'll never forget the first real friend I've ever had.

She lets go, blinking away her tears, and by the time we find our way to the kitchen, the sniffling has stopped, too. I lean against the snow-white counter as she puts away our groceries.

"Until my shitty father slithered off this mortal coil, I thought all the damage he'd done to me, and all the damage I'd done *for* him, was insurmountable. That I'd never be able to climb over it or tunnel under it."

My voice shakes as the past rises to meet me, and I pause to clear my throat.

"He did everything possible to chisel away my edges, to make me dull and round. Pliable. Once I lost all my angles, he molded what was left into a weapon. His weapon, who acted and looked and behaved how he demanded. Who would exact revenge on everybody he felt did him dirty, even though I'm not sure anyone really ever did. The only place I was ever my own was in my head, and even that was touch-and-go sometimes." I absentmindedly take a bite of the raw, peeled carrot Vann shoves in my hand, and the snappy crunch brings me back to the present. "Shit, sorry for the blabbing."

The last bit of vegetable disappears into my mouth, and I take my time chewing it. I choose my next words carefully, knowing they'll leave me exposed and vulnerable.

"Thank you for what you said. That thing about believing in me."

"You're welcome." She continues cleaning and cutting fruit and veggies, dividing them between two plastic containers. "I meant it."

"Nobody's ever believed in me. Except maybe in my ability to destroy everything I touch. Oh, and my stellar liquid liner application skills. That talent is undeniable." I wink and she laughs. "I don't think I've ever had an actual friend."

"Well, you do now." The grin she tosses over her shoulder is wide and honest.

Today's emotional Slip 'N Slide threatens to overwhelm me again and I'm not quite ready to cry in front of anybody twice in one day.

"Okay, friend, I need to ask a favor."

"Uh-huh. And what's the favor?" She rolls her eyes, the smile never leaving her face.

"I know we talked about the whole 'let's teach Hali to cook so she doesn't starve to death or eat her weight in donuts' plan, but would you mind if I went for a walk? I feel like I need some air."

"We can start cooking lessons tomorrow. Go take your walk."

Flashing her a quick, grateful grin, I grab my hoodie and take off out the door.

The weather cleared since we got back, and the late afternoon sun still offers some warmth when it kisses my cheeks. I haven't had a chance to explore the property The Overlook stands on, but I do remember the way the beach called to me that first day, so I head in that direction.

Once I reach to the waterline, I discover a small jetty where the patch of pebbly sand ends and the impassable shoreline begins. A flash of color about halfway out winks in the setting sun, and I pick my way carefully among the coffee table-sized boulders and smaller rocks until I reach the spot.

Glinting up at me is a small, haphazard pile of colored stones. Ranging in size from fingernail-tiny to a hen's egg, each is unique in shades of scarlet, amber, and strangely pretty mottled green. Tucked next to a large, flat slab that looks like a perfect spot to sit and ignore the world, I wonder if their placement was purposeful. A little hidey-hole of hidden beauty I'd never have noticed if the sun hadn't been at the perfect height, and I wasn't standing at just the right angle.

Climbing up onto the rock's surface, I reach down beside it and find one of the larger scarlet pieces. It fits the hollow of my palm, cool and solid, while I sit comfortably cross-legged, staring out at the water. Facing the Sound like this, the cries of the gulls my only company, I tap into a deep calm I didn't know existed within me. As I relax, I tumble the pretty red stone from one hand to the other and back again, and it slowly warms from the heat of my palms. My mind quiets and my heart rate slows.

Until I sense a presence behind me and a resigned sigh falls from my lips.

All good things must end. Even my ten minutes of Zen.

"Agate."

"Bless you?" I say without turning around.

He snorts out a laugh.

"That wasn't a sneeze. It's the name of what's in your hand. Since you found my spot and my stash, you should at least be aware of what you're playing with."

This time it's me that snorts.

"First, how could you possibly know what I have in my hand with my back to you? The only way is if you'd been watching me from the beach when I picked it up."

No response.

"Second, I didn't realize this spot had been claimed

when I sat down, or that the *agate* wasn't here of its own accord."

Okay, so that part is a bit of a lie.

Still no response.

I close my eyes and draw in a big breath of the fresh, clean air. Letting it out slowly, I allow my shoulders to lower and my annoyance at being interrupted to dissipate before standing.

As I turn to face Ty, the breeze picks up and tangles its fingers in my hair. The long chestnut strands lift and twirl in a crazy dance around my head, the setting sun's warm glow turning pieces of it mahogany as they fly in front of my eyes. The moment makes me grin involuntarily, but when I catch a glimpse of him through the swirling mess, his expression shocks the smile from my face.

Fiery lust.

An ache of guilt.

And a soul-deep recognition.

All of it raw, and all of it hidden away as soon as our eyes meet. My nerves sing and my heart picks up a staccato beat. It leaves me feeling unsettled and exposed. With that single look, it's like he laid bare every secret I've never told.

In my haste to escape the emotion threatening to engulf me, I slip as I step down off the tabletop rock, and my ankle rolls painfully. Wincing, I shove the ruby-red piece of agate at Ty.

"Sorry," I mutter.

Moving unsteadily down the jetty toward the sand, I grit my teeth against the pain and tuck my hair behind my ears.

"Hali," he calls, but I don't turn around.

"Won't happen again. Spot and stash are all yours," I yell into the wind and hobble back to my cabin.

the night
lightly swaying

CHAPTER FIFTEEN

Ty

I must have dozed off because the bleating of my phone annoys me awake, and I know who it is without even looking.

Kess has this habit of texting the same way he talks. Instead of a single message, he hits send after each thought or two, resulting in repeated notifications on my end, one right after the other in rapid succession.

I dig my phone out of my pocket and push myself up to a sitting position on the edge of the bed. The incoming messages do nothing to improve my pisstastic mood.

> KESS: You okay, Brother?
>
> KESS: Haven't heard from you and wanted to make sure you haven't been hunted down and hog-tied by some crazed female.
>
> KESS: If you were, and said crazed female is the one reading this, how do I wrangle an invite? I'll bring my own cuffs.
>
> KESS: If this is Ty, expect a call from Steady later. We managed to get you some time away, but the wolves are still hovering just outside the door.
>
> KESS: They want to hammer out the details for the European tour. Steady wants to know what you think you can work with so he can go back to them with something.

I let the phone drop from my hands, not bothering to answer. Any response I give right now will be shitty and I'm not looking to shoot the messenger.

As much as I've grown to love Europe over the past few years, the thought of going back on tour in my current state of mind makes me physically ill. Pompous, money-hungry, and clueless label execs are the worst aspect of this business. They're the last thing I want to deal with right now. 'Those who can't do, teach' is as true in the music industry as anywhere else, but it's more like 'those who can't do, annoy the fuck out of those who can'. The suits always act like they know what's best, often at the expense of running the talent into the ground.

This day just keeps getting better and better.

Scooping the phone up from the floor, I check the time and see I've only got eight minutes until the shuttle leaves the pick-up point. A quick glance in the mirror on my way out startles me, and the prominence of my scowl suggests I might want to pick a new expression. One that looks less like I chew the heads off live animals.

By the time I make it up to the top of the hill, my frustration and unhappiness are tucked away, masked by the carefully crafted public persona I've had to cultivate. It's that skill alone that stifles the string of curses and urge to flee prompted by the sight of the two girls standing beside the SUV.

"Ty! You made it." The blonde—Erissa, I think—bats her spidery lashes in welcome.

"Yeah, well, even rock stars have to eat," I state the obvious and the redhead titters.

"We thought maybe you wouldn't come because of the shitshow in group this morning. Like, maybe you were really upset by how that horrible bitch attacked us for no reason." Sabrina screws her face up in disgust. "I mean, you're a true artist. We understand how sensitive you must be."

Erissa nods in apparent agreement with her friend before they start yammering on about how much they love the latest album.

Over the years I've gotten adept at ignoring background noise, and all the fake fawning from these two is just that...noise. But something must be fucking with my bullshit filter. Even though I'm trying like hell to tune them out, the very fact they exist is setting my teeth on edge.

Thankfully, they hit a brief lull in their conversation, and I pick up the sound of approaching footsteps. Mari's white-blonde hair comes into view, followed by a flash of dark, rich chestnut.

Hali. Mari must've taken what I said to heart and let her stay.

The jolt of pleasure I experience at the realization unnerves me, and I don't like being off-kilter. Thinking fast, I realize I can use the situation to my advantage.

I lean back against the side of the white vehicle and grace each wannabe groupie with a cheeky grin that invites them to drape themselves all over me. And true to form, they take the bait. By the time Mari, Hali, and Vann step onto the driveway, the tableau is arranged to elicit maximum annoyance, and my target's face doesn't disappoint. She may be trying to ignore my presence, but the muscles twitching in her clenched jaw tell me that it isn't working.

Point for me, thank you very much.

I don't get to enjoy my childish little victory though, because she turns the tables on me again.

I step forward with every intention of letting her

know who's responsible for her continued presence here. But before I can say a word, her hand is squeezing my junk through my jeans. Shocked, I can only stand stock-still while she whispers that Mari already told her what I did and that it changes nothing. The pressure of her grip on my dick, the movement of her breath next to my ear, and the sensation of her fantastic tits rubbing against my arm, all render me temporarily mute.

Again.

She chuckles and climbs into the back row of the van, leaving me seething.

Erissa and Sabrina beckon me to join them in the middle row. My only course of action is to carry on with the ruse of enjoying their attention. I grit my teeth and climb in between them, not even buckled in before they're pawing at me.

The only satisfying moment during the ride to town is catching sight of Hali's reflection in the side window of the van. She looks pissed off enough to spit nails.

Good. You don't even understand the rules, Rich Girl, so don't think you can play the game. Score another point for me.

When we finally stop, I pay no attention to Mari calling after me as I stride in the opposite direction from the small grocery store. The wind carries her voice away, leaving me in relative peace. I walk for another few minutes, doing a loop down the main street and cutting back along the path that carves the shoreline. Up ahead, a lone figure is staring out at the water turned gray under a leaden sky. Dark hair in a tempest swirling around her, I recognize the long strands and the deep purple jacket she's wearing right away.

I duck under the eaves of the town post office and try to ignore the slightly pervy feeling peering around one of the pillars gives me. She's too far away to read her expression, but something about her stance speaks to me, whispers of something familiar. It might be the tilt of her jaw or the set of her shoulders, but whatever it is, I need to break the connection. This girl is getting in my head, and that's not good.

Come to think of it, none of this is good. Not the electricity that charges the air whenever she's around, or the effect her body has on mine. And sure as hell not the disconcerting pull I feel toward her on a level deep enough to freak me out a little.

Now that my mood really matches the weather, I shove my hands in my pockets, tearing my eyes away from the girl who has no idea what she's doing to me. I head back toward the grocery store, the scowl already weighing my brow growing heavier with each step.

Unfortunately for Hali, she must've decided to rejoin the others at nearly the same time and ended up fifteen steps in front of me. The delicate and infinitely sexy perfume she seems to favor teases my senses in the brisk air. My balls tighten and my dick twitches.

And just like that, I go from annoyed to severely

pissed off. Whether it's at myself, at her, or at the world is irrelevant. A black mist colors everything, and all I know is I need an outlet. Something to make the incessant buzz of grief and anger and pain stop. Until she's pressed against me in the baking aisle, I have no idea what that actually means.

By the time I undo the button on her jeans, I'm too far gone to give a shit.

You are a complete fucking idiot. What in the holy hell were you thinking?

I spend the ride back to The Overlook alternating between mental self-flagellation and reliving the sensation of my fingers buried in the soft, slick, heat between her legs. The van barely rolls to a stop before she's out the side door at a near-run. Without a word to anybody, I'm not far behind, slamming my cabin door shut hard enough to rattle the framed art hanging on the walls.

The problem is, now that I've managed to escape to the privacy I thought I needed, I realize that it's the last place I want to be. My thoughts are awkward and judgmental companions I have no idea how to deal with.

As if summoned by my shitty mood, Kess's number flashes across the display of my phone.

"Brother. How's summer camp?" he asks when I answer.

"Oh, the usual. Macaroni crafts and Kumbaya." My voice is forced and pitched too high.

"Uh-huh. What's going on?"

"Dude, if I had a clue what the fuck was going on, I wouldn't be in this mess." I drop into the leather recliner with a sigh.

"If there's a mess, there has to be pussy involved. What did you do?"

"Why the hell do you assume *I* did something, asshole?"

"Oh, shit." His low rumble of laughter eases a bit of the pressure from earlier. "You did something, all right. Who is she?"

"Never mind. It doesn't matter. She's a teenage headcase with a chip the size of a Buick on her spoiled rich girl shoulder."

"Damn, Brother. You've got it bad." He laughs again.

"If the only reason you called was to annoy me, you can fuck right off."

"Pfft, I've been annoying you for seventeen years, why the hell would I stop now?"

I shake my head and a grin splits my face as he continues with the reason for his call.

"Mari texted to tell me the prisoners are allowed visitors this weekend. I was going to show up with a willing female or two and offer you a conjugal, but I get the impression you've got that covered," my oldest friend in the world continues.

"Sweet Jesus, the last thing I need is more clingers. There are two of them up here that make me want to take a stroll in traffic."

"Groupies in the boonies? Well, if you aren't going to partake, maybe fun Uncle Kess will show them a good time. I'm always down for a good bush whackin'."

I can imagine the lascivious eyebrow waggle that accompanied his words, and I find myself laughing.

"I take it that means I'll be seeing your ugly face this weekend?"

"Absolutely, Brother. In the meantime, go find your big-chipped lady and convince her to play with your macaroni until you're singing Kumbaya."

the right
lightly sw

CHAPTER SIXTEEN

Ty

*M*y attitude needs a serious adjustment before it gets me into deep shit.

I'm not a shrink, but even I'm qualified to make that diagnosis. I have to find a way to let my grief and resentment go. Grief for the father I lost, and resentment toward the mother I never had. One stayed to raise me and gave both Kess and me every opportunity he could. The other did everything possible to destroy me, to set fire to every shred of hope, every dream I'd ever had.

The cloudy skies from earlier eventually cleared, slanting a beam of dark gold sunlight across the wall opposite the chair I'd been planted in for almost an hour. I needed to sort through my jumbled emotions, so I locked up the cabin and headed down toward the beach.

As soon as I stepped onto the sand, I realized I wasn't alone.

My intention was to apologize for what happened in the grocery store, and for being an asshole in general. But I never got the chance.

She disappeared into the gathering dusk, leaving me alone on the empty beach. Now my chest is banded by an emotion that I don't have the slightest idea what to do with. The small red stone she shoved at me still retains the warmth from her hand, and I clutch it tighter in my palm.

Why do I care? She could be a basket case or an axe murderer or a reporter, for fuck's sake...I don't even know her.

My rational mind may demand logic, but the deepest parts of myself, parts I thought long buried, whisper that I know her better than anyone else I've ever met.

When my feet hit the front steps, it hits me that instinct rather than conscious thought must've carried me back from the beach to the cabin. The path between the two is ingrained in my memory like ruts in a dirt road after years of rain.

The first time I was here, I would spend hours every day down at the water's edge. Nobody bothered me—no ridiculous requests, no demands of my time from the label, and no members of the fairer sex trying to suck my soul dry. It was just me, wrestling with the demons my mother left behind, and the wailing of the gulls as they wheeled out over the Sound.

'The fairer sex' is something my dad always said. Once Heroin Heartbreak made it big, I realized what a ludicrous misnomer the term was. I mean, I've known women who would shank their sisters on the off chance that one of the guys in the band would sweat on them. The words still held humor for me, though, and I'd always grin and roll my eyes when Dad would use them.

Until it wasn't funny anymore.

Because there was nothing fair about the woman who ripped me apart.

"You can't be serious. I'm your son, for fuck's sake. Granted, you abandoned me when I was five, but still, flesh and blood have to count for something." The words rip from my throat in disbelief.

"But Ty, sweetheart, you never would have gotten to where you are now if I hadn't left." She nods, like agreeing with her own bullshit somehow makes it palatable. "You needed me to leave."

"Are you kidding me? I needed you to leave. What the hell kind of person, kind of mother, says shit like that?"

Nothing seems real as I drain the glass of whiskey in my hand. The harsh burn does nothing to slam reality back into me, as the woman perched on the white leather couch leans forward earnestly.

"Just think about it. If I'd stayed, you never would have met Ryan Kessworth. Without him, you never would have had the perseverance to make it. You've always been too much like your father, and we both know he never would have pushed you. If I'd loved you, you would have stayed weak, just like he always was." Her mouth twists unpleasantly. "I needed to force you to experience the pain of my leaving to make you what you are, to set all the little pieces in motion."

"Are you insane?" I take another long swallow of the fiery amber liquid, straight from the bottle this time. She doesn't respond, just sits there slow blinking at me, like a feral cat trying to lull me into submission. "No, answer that, please. It was a legitimate question. Are you insane?"

Blink. Blink.

"All right then, try this one instead. Why did you come back? Why do you think you have a right to be a part of a life you have nothing to do with?"

She dismisses my questions with a wave of her thin, skeleton-like fingers. "Oh Ty, you've got the wrong impression. I don't want to be a part of your life."

Now I'm the one blinking at her, only in straight-up confusion. She laughs—a fake, plastic, high-pitched chuckle.

"I don't want anything to do with you. I just want what's

rightfully mine." Her nicotine-stained teeth appear between her over-lined raspberry red lips in a gruesome grin. "As I said, you wouldn't be where you are without me, so you owe me for that. I think half a million should do. For now."

Am I hallucinating? This conversation can't be happening.

I choke on the audacity of her words and chase them with a third of the bottle in my hand before responding.

"Rightfully yours? What the fuck are you talking about? You think I should pay you for being a fucking douchebag?" The laugh that rumbles out of me is unexpected and callous,

Her demeanor changes immediately, and any last hint of pleasantry is dropped. The cruelty and craziness float to her surface, unmasked, naked, and pissed off.

"Listen to me very carefully Tyler. Do you like your life? Are you enjoying the money and pussy and adoration? Because I can make it all disappear real quick." She snaps her fingers for emphasis. "You and your father will pay one way or another." The mask slides back across her features, her entire body suddenly taking on the shape and form of an innocent victim. Her hands twist together before one flutters to her throat, her voice soft and plaintive. "My life with him was so awful, Your Honor—I had to run from my husband to save my life. The abuse was constant, and the mental scars rival the physical ones he left behind." She trembles when she pushes up the sleeve of her ill-fitting sweatshirt, revealing a ladder of thin white scars interspersed with the white moons of old burns. "He cut me. Used my body as an ashtray."

Blink, blink.

"What in the actual fuck are you doing?" Watching her simper while she spews vitriol about my father makes me sick to my stomach. My rational mind understands full well she's lying her face off, but the performance is shockingly well done.

"I couldn't save my son. My husband raised him to be just as cruel as he was. Now that my poor, damaged, boy is famous, I've seen the women who lust after him and I had to come forward. To save them from the ugliness that lives in my offspring, save them from what I endured." Her voice trembles and a single, fat, crocodile tear slides down her cheek.

The absurdity of her statements pushes me to near-hysterics. But the calculated smirk that hovers around the corners of her mouth delivers a sobering gut punch that almost turns me inside out.

Fame is a fickle thing. You can be the darling of the industry, with fans clamoring just to be near you. But all it takes to flatten that house of cards is one tiny seed of doubt planted by somebody who appears marginally credible. And who's more credible than a parent? She could be proven to be bat-shit crazy after the fact, but it won't matter. Because the shadow will be cast, lives will be ruined, and the question of 'what if' will linger.

Her smug grin stretches into a full-fledged sneer the second she sees the truth hit home for me.

This woman has the power to shatter everything I've worked for, everything Kess has worked for. The power to destroy my father. I can't let that happen, and she's fully aware of that.

I down another three swallows from the bottle and fumble for my phone.

An electronic trill breaks through the dense fog of memory, and I reach for the device in my back pocket.

"Steady, please tell me you have good news."

"Ty, it's good to hear your voice. How are things up north?"

"Peachy. Mari pretty much called me a man-whore, and I'm ninety-three percent certain I'm losing my mind."

"Okay, who is she?".

"What the hell is it with you and Kess? Who said anything about a she?" His assumption annoys me.

"Oh, there's definitely a she."

Amusement is clear in his tone. Steady is one of the greatest guys I've ever met. We owe him so much. But I swear to God, this conversation is pissing me off and right now I would happily kick him in the nuts.

"Tell me what the label said. Kess warned me this call was coming, and I can already tell I'm not going to like the answer, so you might as well just say it."

"Twelve days." He drops his bomb and waits for my response.

"Twelve days?" The words are pitched low, even though inside I'm seething and want to scream. "My father dies, I check into The Overlook, and the fucking label has decided everything is going to be all better in *twelve days?*"

"I'm sorry, kid. I wish I could do more. The label wants what they want. At least the European leg is short, only twenty dates, so it'll be quick and dirty. Four weeks tops. Once it's over, you can take some real time to get your head right." His tone echoes a fraction of the frustration that's making it hard for me to think. "I'm sure Mari will welcome you back. Or we can find a nice vacation house to rent on a deserted island somewhere. No label, no paps, just you and your demons."

"Fine, whatever. It's not like I have much of a choice, is it?" I scrub my hand over my face, pausing to rub my temple for a second. "Look, I have to go. I'll talk to you later."

Disconnecting the call without another word, I suck in an angry breath. It takes every ounce of willpower I have to not hurl my phone into the trees before stomping up the stairs and slamming the cabin door shut behind me.

CHAPTER SEVENTEEN

Hali

The morning of my first one-on-one therapy session is bright and crisp—the polar opposite of my dark and sluggish mood.

"You'll be fine, I promise," Vann swears, her small hands dwarfed by the giant coffee mug clutched between them.

"I'm pretty sure you said something similar about group and look how well that turned out." I'm focused on tying my shoelaces so she can't see my eyes roll, but I do it anyway.

"Just go and talk it out." She yawns. "Hey, do you have anybody coming for visitor's day tomorrow?"

My sharp laugh widens her eyes.

"If you only understood how ridiculous that question really is…" I grab my jacket, give her a mock salute and let the door swing shut behind me.

I'm a walking thunderhead, all gray and grumbly, shot through with the occasional jolt of angry lightning. I hadn't thought about there being family days here. When Vann mentioned it, my natural outward reaction was dismissive bravado. Now that I'm alone, I let myself admit what I'm really feeling.

Angry.

Sad.

Discarded.

Because I'm one hundred percent certain there's not a chance in hell anybody is showing up here to visit me tomorrow or any other day.

And I need to find a way to be okay with it because it's my own fault.

Slipping through the back doors of the main lodge, I follow the discreet directional placards on the walls to my psychologist's office.

Suite 107. Here we go.

Before I can knock on the frosted glass door, it swings wide.

"Good morning, Hali." Mari's smile is welcoming.

"I don't think I'd go that far," I grumble. "But, seriously? *You're* my therapist?"

Undaunted by my rudeness, she beckons me inside.

"You could do worse." She shrugs.

Without bothering to respond, I slouch into one of the comfortable leather chairs on either side of a small glass coffee table. Mari takes a seat in the other and tucks one leg up under the other. My anxiety about this whole process forces me to speak first, and to be bitchy about it.

"I hope you don't think I'm going to sit here and spill all of my secrets, because sorry, Mari, that's not how it works. You may have a piece of paper hanging on the wall that says you're qualified to diagnose my darkness, but paper's cheap. Up until a few days ago, I didn't know you from Adam and I'm not comfortable turning myself inside out for your dissection."

Speech over, I resist the urge to shift in my chair while she studies me in silence. Fidgeting is a sign of weakness, my father used to say. A chink in your armor, and easy for an enemy to exploit. While I don't view Mari as an enemy, I wouldn't call her a friend either. But then, I've long been conditioned to view everybody as a foe.

"You don't have to talk about anything you don't want to." She snags a colorfully wrapped bundle from the small glass bowl on the coffee table. "The longer you keep it all in though, the more it's going to fester." She pops the candy in her mouth. "But it's your dime, as they say. We can just sit here and stare at each other."

Her nonchalance is both comforting and disconcerting at the same time. Even though she doesn't say another word, just picks up her notebook and pen, the insecure child in me reads her silence as reproachful. I have no idea if it's real or imagined, but it gets my back up regardless.

"Does this tactic really work?"

Tucking a stray strand of hair behind her ear, she raises her eyes to mine, all placid innocence.

"What tactic would that be?"

"The one where you make me feel like shit and goad me into talking by staying silent."

Her answering smile couldn't be more angelic if it was worn by St. Peter himself, but the devil dances in her eyes. It's manipulation at its finest, but I respect the attempt and decide to throw her a bone.

"Fine," I huff dramatically, crossing my arms like a shield and slouching further in my chair. "Ask your damn questions."

She's won this particular battle, but at least she doesn't rub it in. Instead, she taps her pen against her bottom lip before speaking. Almost like she realizes she's not going to convince me to talk about everything she thinks I should right now, so she's trying to decide what to poke at first.

"Why did you agree to come to The Overlook, Hali?"

The question is so simple, so easy, so damn normal, yet it hammers the panic button and I immediately start looking for a way to divert her focus.

Mari's office is very much like she is—casual and cozy, while still being classy. One wall is covered by floor-to-ceiling bookcases, and another in framed black and white photographs. I decide the pictures are my best bet. Ignoring the question she hung in the air between us, I ask one of my own.

"Are you some sort of photographer or something?"

"Or something."

The images intrigue me, so I move closer for a better look. Based on the hair and clothing styles, I'd guess some of them go back twenty or thirty years, and almost all of them seem to be either musicians or touristy land-marks. I don't recognize many of the faces or places at first, but then a smaller frame grabs my attention, the photo it holds making my belly flutter.

"Did you take this?" I ask, not turning around, and she answers without me having to point out which one.

"No. A lot of those were taken by my uncle, including that one."

The photo had to have been taken at the same time as the video, only after Ty realized he was being filmed. He's still sitting on the edge of a stage, acoustic guitar balanced on his lap. This time he's acknowledged the camera, but even with the smirk tucking the corner of his lips into one cheek, an ache echoes in his eyes. I turn back to face Mari.

"You know Ty, then. I mean, outside of here." It's more a statement than a question, but I still mentally kick myself for showing any interest.

"I do." She nods. "Does that bother you?"

"Why would I care?" I ignore the tiny flare of jealousy in the pit of my stomach. "Isn't it some sort of conflict of interest or whatever?"

"I'm not his therapist, and when he's here, he's a client. End of story."

"Why did you become a shri—sorry, a *psychologist*? You could probably do a thousand other things with your life."

"My uncle, the same one that took those photos, works in the music industry. He started getting me concert tickets and backstage passes when I was around twelve or so." She sits a little straighter, pride in her work apparent in the set of her chin. "I always tell him my chosen career is all his fault. So many of my favorite bands self-destructed from the lifestyle and their own demons. I wanted to help." She shrugs. "Becoming a psychologist and opening The Overlook seemed like the best way to do that."

"Wait, you own this place? Like, own it, own it?" I don't even try to keep the grudging respect from my voice.

With a nod, she motions to the chair across from her.

"You learned something about me, so how about you share something about yourself?"

"Whatever."

I toss my hair and sit back down. The silver-faced clock on the desk ticks away the seconds as the silence between us grows longer. The rapid pace of my anxious heartbeat starts to slow, and I find myself relaxing almost against my will. The words leave my lips before I can stop them.

"I wish I knew what I did to deserve this fucked up life. What I did to deserve my father."

CHAPTER EIGHTEEN

Hali

"Tell me about him," Mari encourages patiently.

I lean back against the chair and close my eyes, finding it more comfortable than trying to maintain eye contact. "When I was little, I remember kids being dropped off at school by their parents. Parents who obviously loved them. Faces wreathed in smiles, hugs and kisses goodbye, and cookies in brightly colored lunch bags." I wince at the memory. "Except for me. I always had the man I feared the most dropping me off."

"Why do you think he was always the one with drop-off duty?"

"Besides the fact that my mother pretended I didn't exist, I'm pretty sure he did it to keep tabs on me. Looking back, even then he couldn't seem to handle not knowing what I was doing. He constantly monitored my interactions with the other kids, especially The Heirs."

"The Heirs?" Confusion is apparent in her voice.

"The children of the elite, the founding families of the town I grew up in. He was obsessed with them in a way that quickly became creepy and inappropriate. He was obvious about it, didn't even try to hide his interest."

"That must have been hard for you." Paper crinkles as her pen moves over the pages of her notebook.

"The few invitations I used to receive, stopped altogether. Parents would turn and walk the other way if they caught a glimpse of him. Kids wouldn't sit anywhere near me in class or at lunch, and eventually, my teachers stopped trying to force the issue. People were either terrified of or weirded out by my father, and because of that, they had no idea what to do with me." I'm glad my eyes are still closed, so I don't have to deal with the pity I'm sure is all over Mari's face. Drawing in a deep, albeit shaky, breath, I continue.

"Loneliness and shame became my constant companions and bled into every single relationship I had left. My existence was toxic and terrifying at home, so I took all my hostility out on the people around me at school. Which of course, is exactly what my father wanted to happen. He made that clear many times."

"Why do you think he behaved the way he did?" The question is followed by more pen scratching.

"Because he was crazier than a shithouse rat?" I snort. "He was built of blind rage and fueled by insanity and the desire to win at all costs. The man's blistering temper and wild outbursts were legendary. It's like after he realized that the founding families would never grant him access, never welcome him with open arms, he just said 'fuck it' and let himself go utterly nuts. Any calm or chill or grace he might have been faking slipped away like so much mud down the hillside." Moisture leaks from the corners of my eyes and traces lazy paths down my temples, but I don't reach to wipe it away.

"How did all of that affect you?" The next question comes with a tissue pressed into my hand. That small show of compassion widens the cracks in my armor.

"Things started to really go downhill when I was about thirteen. Kids at school would recoil from me, parting like the Red Sea when I walked down the hall. Nobody liked me, and it hurt." My short, sharp laugh rings with painful truth. "I wanted friends and parties and dates, but..." I twine my hands together and dig my nails into the soft flesh of my palms. "The knife edge my father had me balancing on threatened to cleave me in two. I started doing crazy things, even crazier than he demanded. All in hopes that somebody would ask me what was happening at home, but nobody ever did." The tears are flowing for real now, so I open my eyes and sit up straight, scrubbing at my wet cheeks with the tissue.

Mari doesn't speak at first. She just pushes the whole box of tissues across the table in my direction and gives me a minute to collect myself.

"Do you think you can continue?" Her voice is gentle, filled with genuine kindness, and it irritates me like a day-old mosquito bite. Because I don't deserve it.

"Look, I realize I'm an awful person. How many horrible things I've said and done." I try not to sniffle. "You don't have to pretend to give a shit just because you're my therapist." I lower my eyes and make a point of studying a strategically placed rip in the leg of my jeans.

"I don't believe you're an awful person, Hali. You were an abused child forced to do awful things by somebody who was supposed to love you, not exploit you."

She waits for me to say something, but the words won't budge around the lump in my throat. I just keep staring at the frayed edges, so she continues.

"Did you like doing those things?"

That snaps my head up fast enough to give me whiplash.

"Hell, no. What the fuck kind of question is that?" The suggestion that I might have taken pleasure in the things I did disgusts me.

"An honest one. If you didn't enjoy it, why did you do it?"

"He was always watching me." I all but whisper. "If I did something he didn't like, if I went against his wishes, he'd make sure to show me how angry he was." My skin crawls and I clear my throat. "He never really wanted to be a part of them. I don't think his ego would have ever allowed it. He had to be better, had to have more. When he was forced to accept that would never happen, he wanted to destroy them, and his plan was to use me to do it."

"Doesn't that suggest who the awful person in the equation really was?"

"You can't say that. You have no idea what I've done." Tiny droplets of cold sweat coat my lower back. "I have a half-sister I didn't know existed until this year—born of rape and greed. When she showed up in Folkestone, she had no idea what she was getting into." I choke back the bile rising in my throat. "Instead of welcoming her, I bullied her. I convinced the town fuck-up to slip something in her drink at a party. To take her to the same dank, dirty, broken down, old barn she was conceived in." Hot tears streak my cheeks. "I cut her hair off," I wail. "He assaulted her, left bite marks on her thighs...her breasts. I stopped him, but he tried to-to-to..." Vomit fills my mouth, spewing onto my lap before I can stop it.

Ashamed and distressed, I'm frozen in place. The only thing that I seem to be able to do is keep whispering "I'm sorry" over and over.

"It's okay, Hali, you're all right." Mari grabs handfuls of tissues from the box and moves in front of me, wiping at my jeans. "Just breathe for me." She gives my hand a squeeze. "You're okay." She tosses the soggy wad into the wastebasket and picks up her phone. A minute later there's a tap on the door, and whoever is outside hands her a wet washcloth and a small towel.

The cloth is warm against my skin. Soothing. By the time I use the towel to dry my face and wipe off the bit of puke stuck in the ends of my hair, my tears have all but stopped.

"I'm sorry about the mess."

"No, I'm sorry," Mari gives me a sad smile. "Your physical reaction to our conversation was unexpected. I didn't understand the depth of what happened to you and I shouldn't have pushed so hard."

I'm grateful for her apology, but all I can do is nod, my system still in overload.

Another tap at the door, and this time it's Vann on the other side, a pair of light gray sweatpants and my pink hoodie clutched to her chest.

"Miss Henderson asked me to bring these?" Her puzzled expression fades to compassion as soon as she sees me.

"Vann, can you please walk Hali back to your cabin after she changes?" Mari turns to face me again. "That was scary and awful, but it was also something for you to be proud of. That's the first time you've ever talked about any of this?"

"Yes," is all I can muster.

"I'm proud of you." Seeming to ignore my puke-spattered clothes, she leans in and gives me a quick hug before patting my roommate's arm and excusing herself.

"So, remember when you said therapy wouldn't be that bad?" I give my roommate a big, game show flourish, emphasizing the mess on my jeans. "Ta-daaaa."

"Hali, I'm so sor—"

"I know, I know. I'm sorry, you're sorry, Mari's sorry. I just want to change and go hide in the cabin. We can play the blame game later." I soften my words with a wink and a watery smile and reach for the clothes she brought with her.

CHAPTER NINETEEN

Hali

We haven't left the cabin in two days. That therapy session was rough, and it dredged up a lot of things I'm afraid to look too hard at. Mari called a few times to check in, and when I requested a couple of days to recover, she agreed.

As a distraction, Vann's been giving me cooking lessons. Unsurprisingly, I'm not the most stellar student, but I enjoy spending time with her. We made chocolate and butterscotch chip pancakes yesterday morning and delicious butter chicken for dinner. Since I didn't set anything on fire, I'll take it as a win.

The tantalizing scent of bacon and the sound of K-pop karaoke finally coax me out of our room, even though I'd be happy to sleep all day.

Last night was a long one.

I woke up shortly after one a.m. to Vann sitting on

the side of my bed shaking me. Apparently, I started talking in my sleep, jumbled nonsense at first, but it quickly escalated into violent thrashing and hysterical begging for somebody to stop. By the time she got me totally awake, panic was squeezing the breath from my lungs and both of our faces were streaked with tears. Rather than try to go back to sleep, she stayed up with me, both of us huddled on my bed watching eighties rom-coms on my laptop until the sun came up.

Laughter bubbles up through my grogginess when I walk into the kitchen. In the midst of dishing up bacon and scrambled eggs, Vann is singing horribly and shaking her ass along to Dynamite. She hands me a plate with a twirl and motions me to the table.

"A little BTS for lunch today?" I tease.

Her face lights up as she reaches to turn down the speaker on her phone.

"You know who BTS is? You're not a musical heathen after all." She claps in animated glee.

"Don't get too excited. That's the only song from them I recognize, so I'm pretty sure I still qualify as a heathen."

She shakes her head and joins me at the table. I glance up at her as we eat, and wonder, not for the first time, how I got lucky enough to be paired with her here. I don't think I could have picked a better friend. But while she's funny and smart and kind, she's hiding a few demons of her own. Maybe one day she'll trust me enough to talk to me about them, and I can try to help her like she's been helping me. Without her, I'm not sure I'd be able to handle the terrifying things being unearthed from my psyche. Since my therapy session with Mari, other memories long-buried out of self-preservation, have come screaming back to the surface.

Like my nightmare last night.

I told Vann I didn't remember anything about it, that it was just a random dream.

I lied.

The night swallows me, heavy and cloying. My breath hitches, little whimpers coming along for the ride. Daddy says only babies and weaklings need nightlights and he won't allow them. The shadows in this house have always been filled with teeth, but lately I've been having more trouble than usual shutting my eyes against them. I slip out from under my covers and tiptoe to the small desk where my unicorn lamp sits. Clicking it on, I scurry back to bed and dive in. The soft glow pushes back the dark and sleep finally finds me.

I'm wrenched awake by Daddy's pinched face looming over me. Eyes wild, he grabs the end of one of my long braids and drags me out of bed by the hair.

"You want to find out what happens to disobedient children, Hali? I saw the light under your door. How dare you think you can fool me," he seethes.

My scalp stings and I cry out, but rather than let go, he yanks me out of my room and down the hall. My little legs can't keep up with the stride of his much longer ones, and I stumble and fall. It doesn't slow him down, though. If anything, it enrages him even more. He reaches down and grabs me, one spider-like pale hand gripping my tiny bicep hard enough to make me wince, the other grabbing the waistband of my pajama bottoms. The seam of the cotton pants wedges so hard between my legs that I'm sure I'm going to split in two.

I bite down hard on the inside of my lower lip, tasting coppery blood. If I release the wail building in me from the excruciating pain he's causing, that blood won't be the worst thing in my mouth. Daddy keeps special bars of soap that burn my lips and tongue when he needs to wash the devil out.

My heart pounds so hard that I'm worried it might explode in a great big red mess.

We get to the end of the hall, him half-carrying, half-dragging me. The door here is thinner and a little shorter than the others and always locked. Letting go of my pajamas, he reaches in his pocket for the key. When the narrow, steep staircase is revealed, my knees buckle. He grabs my hair again and uses it like the handle on a wagon, pulling me along behind him. My feet scrabble for purchase on the stairs, but I can't keep up and my shins and ankles bang off nearly every step on the way up.

At the top, he tosses me onto the creaky wooden floorboards and my behind hits the ground hard, sending a cloud of dust and dirt swirling into the hot, stale, air. The attic is the scariest place I've ever been, and I've never been up here at night. In the dark, evil lives up here, tangled in the cobwebs and feeding the things that skitter in the shadows.

"We'll break you of your disobedience and your need for a nightlight, Hali, and we'll do it tonight."

"No Daddy, please don't leave me up here. I'm sorry, I won't disobey. I won't turn the light on again, I swear," I beg, frantically trying to grab onto his pant legs and hoist myself up.

"I don't believe you, Hali. You're a baby and a liar. You sit up here and think about how much of a disappointment you are." He kicks me away.

Whimpering and clutching my knees to my thin chest, I take in the room around me with wide, frightened, eyes. Daddy turns and starts down the stairs.

"Don't worry, you'll be better for it, and I expect a 'thank you' in the morning. I won't have an ungrateful brat in my house."

My teeth chatter while I wait for the door close behind him, but before it does, he flicks the switch at the bottom of the stairs.

Full dark drops like a hammer.

"Daddy, no!" The scream erupts before I can stop it and terror takes hold of me. Warmth spreads between my legs as I

wet myself. Tears streak my cheeks, and my breath is wild as absolute fear reverberates through me.

Little claws scratch in the walls and I imagine the mice that live up here scolding me just like Daddy did. I freeze, afraid if I reach out a hand something might reach back, and the puddle of urine is making my pajama pants stick to my legs. Unable to make out my own hand in front of my face, I'm forced to rely on my other senses to find my way around. Sliding my knees under me, I crawl slowly on all fours toward where I think there's a window. If it has curtains, I might be able to open them and let some moonlight in. At least enough to let me see the outline of the room. Something jitterbugs across the back of my hand, and I stifle a scream. I can't convince my shudder-wracked body to move any further, so I curl up in a ball and pray for daylight.

"Hali? Hey, Hals, you okay?" Vann grabs my wrist and gives it a shake, pulling me back to the present.

"Yeah, sorry. Just tired."

My smile is meant to reassure her, but given how low her eyebrows dip in response, I don't think it's working.

"You don't look so good."

Probably because I can still taste the mind-numbing fear

of being locked in the attic, can still remember how he looked at me.

I was only five that first time and I still knew something in his eyes was wrong. Almost inhuman. And it only got worse.

"I'm fine, I swear. See? Eating." I spear a forkful of eggs and swallow them with a cheesy grin plastered across my lips.

She looks like she doesn't quite believe me, but she lets it go.

"We need to leave the cabin today. Get some sunshine on your pasty face."

"*My* pasty face?" I laugh and toss the last corner of my toast at her. "I'm from California, dude. I haven't been pasty a day in my life."

"Oh sure, rub it in," she snorts. "For real though, we need some fresh air. I know it's visitor's day, but everybody usually stays up at the main lodge."

My stomach sinks at the reminder.

"Nobody's coming to visit me, but I don't want to keep you from your family." I clear the table to keep from having to meet her eyes.

"Family. That's a good one." She joins me at the sink. "My mother is too busy saving the world to worry about saving her daughter, and unless there's a free bar, my stepfather isn't interested." Her voice cracks. "Mari has banned him anyway."

I can tell there's a hell of a lot more to that story, but

that's an unpacking for another day. I'm not interested in upsetting Vann right now.

"Then it's just you and me today. Where do you want to go?"

"Oh! I know the perfect spot." She bounces on her tiptoes in excitement. "A neat little glade about fifteen minutes from here. Nobody ever goes there. It's beautiful during the day with the way the sun comes through the trees. And in the evening, it's even better—it has a fire pit."

"Did you just use the words *neat* and *glade* in the same sentence?" I tease, and she snaps a tea towel at me. "I'm kidding, geez. It sounds great."

<hr>

Vann locks the cabin door and hands me the folded blankets she insisted we bring, while she slings the small soft-sided cooler over her shoulder. We pass Ty's cabin and hang a left at the next branch in the path. A handful of people are clustered on the back porch of the main lodge and their chatter filters down to us before being snatched away on the breeze.

It dawns on me that I haven't seen Ty since the jetty. That shouldn't bother me, but part of me misses the friction between us, even if he is an egotistical ass.

I wonder who's coming to visit him today. He probably

has a great family and any number of adoring friends who jump at any chance to spend time with him.

My steps must have slowed because when I look up, Vann's quite a distance ahead. Shaking off thoughts of the rock star next door, I pick up the pace and close the gap between my roommate and me.

The path enters the tree line just ahead, and when we step into the woods it's like entering a whole different world. Small birds with pretty brown and lemon-yellow markings flit from tree to bush and back again. I have no idea what kind they are, but their high, thin, whistles are somehow relaxing.

We traipse ahead for another ten minutes or so and then I figure we must be getting close because Vann's more excited with each step. She keeps jogging ahead, then stops and practically vibrates while waiting for me to catch up.

"You're going to love it here. It's the perfect place to just relax and rechar—" Her words come to as abrupt a halt as she does when she steps into the small clearing.

"Good lord, give me some warning when you're going to hit the brakes," I joke, almost crashing into her.

She doesn't respond, just turns and gives me a pained look before stepping to the side.

"Hello, ladies." A tall, extremely good-looking guy

unfolds himself from a makeshift log bench on the other side of the fire pit. "Care to join us?" The sun catches the blonde in his hair, setting it alight, and his smile is dazzling.

His buddy turns to face us from where he sits on the other bench and smirks.

Of course, Ty is out here in the middle of Vann's glade on visitor's day, because why wouldn't he be? I swear, the Universe hates me.

The whole situation, from his expression to the spike in my pulse, annoys me and I start stomping back the way we came. When a strong hand grabs my arm from behind, I react without thinking and drop our blankets. Spinning around, my fist connects with bone before I trip over my own feet and fall flat on my ass.

CHAPTER TWENTY

Ty

You'd think the prospect of seeing friends and family for an afternoon would make people happy. My last stint here taught me it tends to do the opposite. Anxiety, dread, and anger run rampant in the lead-up to visiting days. It's the odd Overlook resident that actually looks forward to them.

I'm one of the odd ones.

Over the course of the average four-week stay, there are three designated visitor's days. Kess came to every one of them the last time I was here, and he's already made it clear he'll be here today. His good-natured, laid-back attitude and raunchy sense of humor are always what the psychologist ordered. I couldn't ask for a better support system—a better best friend—than him.

Showered and dressed, I find myself staring out of

the kitchen window while I drink my coffee, wondering if the girls are going to finally emerge.

It's been exceptionally quiet around here for the past two days. There's been no activity in or out of their cabin since they scurried back the other morning. The bedroom blinds have stayed closed, and there's been no gravel crunching underfoot or female voices passing by.

The only reason I'm sure they're in the cabin at all is the scent of food that keeps drifting in this direction. Yesterday morning it was chocolate laced with a hint of caramel. Last night it was warm spices that reminded me of my favorite curry restaurant in London.

My stomach growls as I drop two pieces of bread into the toaster, almost like it's whining about getting stuck with the basics. I skim through random emails on my phone and devour my breakfast, washing it down with the last mouthful of coffee. Kess texts me that he's ten minutes out, so I shove my feet into lug-soled, black leather boots, grab my coat, and head up to meet him.

The main lodge is buzzing when I walk in the back doors. People mill around looking uncomfortable, plastic cups of juice and soda clutched like life preservers in a sea of awkward. At least famous faces are pretty common around this place, so nobody makes a big deal out of me being here. I nod and smile in polite greeting and thread my way over to Mari on the other side of the room.

"What do you think it's going to be this time?" she asks with a quiet chuckle.

"I have no idea. I can't say I'd be surprised if he parachuted in."

My grin widens at the thought of my best friend and his penchant for making entrances people rarely forget. I step out onto the porch, Mari right behind me. She explodes into peals of laughter as a flash of color turns off the highway and starts down the winding driveway.

"Oh my God." Her sides are shaking.

It's contagious, and by the time the car rolls to a stop in front of us, we're laughing so hard we can barely breathe.

The driver's door of the hot pink, seventies-era, Cadillac Fleetwood opens and Kess steps out, The Fabulous Thunderbirds' 'Tuff Enuff' blaring from the car stereo.

"Brother." He spreads his arms wide. "Isn't she beautiful?"

"That's one word for her," I jog down the steps and engulf my oldest friend in a bear hug that he returns with a few pounds on my back for good measure.

Mari pushes me out of the way and throws her arms around his neck. He lifts her easily and twirls her around once before setting her back on her feet.

"Turn off your music and park your boat. I mean, could it be any longer?" she teases.

"I aim to please, and the ladies like 'em long." He winks, and she punches him in the shoulder.

"Gross. I don't want to hear about your sex life." The stern expression she's wearing is tempered by the laughter in her voice.

"That's only because you have no idea what you're missing." His eyebrows jump suggestively, and she can't hold back her grin.

"Sure, let's go with that." She snorts. "I have to go make the rounds. It's great to see you, Kess. Be good, you two."

She takes the porch steps two at a time and disappears through the front doors.

***

We manage to square the car away by taking up two spots and parking at an angle. Kess pulls a cooler and portable speaker from the trunk. Before I can ask, he's already answering me.

"I'm like a Boy Scout, Brother. Always prepared." He hands me the speaker. "Tunes fully charged. Off to the usual spot?"

I nod and we head for the path, even though part of me wants to stay back and wait for everybody to leave. I'm sure the uptight masses will do a double take when they find the pink behemoth nestled in amongst their luxury sedans and SUVs.

"You look better, Ty. Still ugly as fuck, of course, but better."

"Gee, thanks. And yeah, I'm starting to feel more like myself…"

"Buuuuuut?"

"Nothing. It's good. I'm good. For the most part," I shrug.

He looks like he wants to dig, but we step into the clearing, and I distract him by designating him the DJ. It works for about three minutes. Once he's comfortable on the bench across from me, cold soda in his hand, all bets are off.

"Before I hit play on the stellar playlist created by your truly, I'm going to need the deets."

"*The deets*? What are you, eleven?" I snort.

He takes that as a signal to continue.

"Who is she?"

"For fuck's sake, why do you think there's a she?"

"For the same reason you suck at playing poker—it's written all over your face." He grins.

"Asshole."

"Call me whatever you want, but you know I'm right. Remember that night in Hamburg, with the roadies and those thr—" He stops and stands, a huge smile blooming across his face. "Hello, ladies. Care to join us?"

I squeeze my soda can and dent it on both sides.

For fuck's sake.

My gut knows who it is. I twist in my seat, and sure enough, Hali's staring daggers at me.

She doesn't say a word, just spins on her heel and takes off in a huff back the way the two of them came. Before my brain registers what my body is doing, I drop the soda and run after her, grabbing her by the arm when I catch up.

That was my first mistake.

The second was not ducking.

As soon as my hand makes contact with her bicep, she drops the bundle in her arms, pivots sloppily, and punches me in the jaw before losing her balance and falling on her butt.

"What the hell was that for?" I rub the side of my face that's stinging like hell. Kess's belly laugh echoes through the clearing, and I know it's aimed at me getting clocked by a girl. To make myself feel better I'm about to make a snide comment about it being karma that dumped her on her ass when her expression stops me. "Shut up, Kess," I yell without turning my head, and my tone silences him immediately.

"Hali, it's okay. I didn't mean to startle you." I slowly crouch down in front of her, maintaining eye contact the whole time.

She's sitting on the path, legs splayed, palms planted behind her. Her position isn't what concerns me, though —the abject terror carved across her frozen features is.

"Hey, it's only me. I won't hurt you."

She doesn't move.

I try a different tack and toss her a cocky grin.

"That's one hell of a right hook you've got. If you wanted my attention, all you had to do was ask. No need for violence."

My words have the desired effect and the color rushes back to her cheeks. She blinks a few times and gives me a sugar-sweet closed-lip smile before kicking my shin out from under me.

There's something amusing about the exchange, and I snicker at the two of us sitting in the middle of the path like little kids. She studies my face for a few seconds, and this time whatever she finds allows her to chuckle in return.

"Sorry about that. You shouldn't sneak up on people," she offers by way of apology.

"I'm just glad you have shitty aim." I rub my jaw again.

"Trust me, if I'd been aiming, you'd be missing a few teeth right now."

"Duly noted."

We sit in a strange silence for a handful of seconds, awkward and comforting at the same time. She openly peruses my face, and it's almost as intimate as a touch. I take the opportunity to admire the way her bottom lip curves into a hint of a natural pout.

"Would you two like to share with the class?" Kess

walks over and offers a hand to each of us, pulling us to our feet.

"Thank—"

My gratitude is effectively silenced by the finger he presses roughly against my mouth.

"I don't believe I've had the pleasure, darlin'. Ryan Kessworth, lead guitarist for Heroin Heartbreak, and best friend to this one." He jerks his head in my direction and shoots Hali one of his megawatt grins.

"Hali Torsten, work in progress, and knee-er of that one's nutsack."

Kess and Vann glance at me with their eyebrows raised and laughter on their lips.

"Reeeally," the one who's supposed to be on my side drawls. "I knew there were shenanigans going on up here." He tucks one arm through Hali's and the other through Vann's, escorting them both to the benches. "Tell Uncle Kess everything." Looking back over his shoulder, he winks, making me grin and shake my head.

right
light   swi

CHAPTER TWENTY-ONE

Ty

I hand over the blankets, retrieved from where they fell, and she takes them with a hesitant smile before jamming them between her and Vann on the bench they're sharing.

An awkward silence descends while everybody looks at me. I stand in front of them all like an idiot, hands in the pockets of my jeans, not quite sure what to do with myself.

Good lord, you perform on stage in front of stadiums packed full of screaming fans, and you can't even figure out what to say to two teenage girls.

Thank God for Kess. He lets me stand there for a few seconds longer, clearly enjoying my discomfort before he finally takes pity on my tongue-tied ass and starts talking.

He's always had this innate ability to make people

comfortable and diffuse even the most volatile situation. There's been the odd time when that diffusion has been delivered by his fist, but he's made it clear he prefers words to punches. He makes it his mission to live up to his mantra of 'I'm a lover, not a fighter'. If life had taken a different path, he would have made an excellent shrink. Or gigolo.

The image of my best friend as a kept man has me snickering when I drop onto to the bench beside him, and some of the tension surrounding our foursome dissipates.

Rather than participate in the conversation that has started to flow between him and Vann, I choose to observe. His presence is coaxing unexpected humor from the girl who until now, I haven't heard say more than three sentences combined. The two of them trade barbs with ease once she's certain nobody here is on the attack.

I've known girls like her. The ones who have no idea what they bring to the table because they don't know there *is* a table. At some point in their lives, they were made to feel so small by cruelty or trauma or their own self-doubt, that nobody has a chance to get to know them and the world misses out. If nothing else comes from spending the afternoon out here, I'm glad Kess could make her feel seen.

Hali listens to their banter and responds with a smile or the occasional laugh, but for the most part, she's an observer like me. Subtly biting her lip and clasping and unclasping her hands gives me the impression she's out of her element, which seems odd for a girl like her. The asshole in me would love to believe that she's star-struck, but that doesn't seem like her style.

Vann is arguing with Kess about rock or pop being the better musical genre when Hali stands and casually plucks one of the blankets beside her.

The clearing we're in is a decent size, probably forty feet wide and twice that long, with the majority of it overhung with trees. A short distance from the benches is a flat section carpeted in thick moss and haphazard clumps of grass, and totally open to the blue sky above. Hali takes her blanket and spreads it out there, before coming back to dig through their cooler for a bottle of apple juice and a sandwich bag of cookies.

Her roommate pauses mid-thought to give her a questioning look, like an unspoken ask if she's okay, to which she nods and smiles.

Vann goes back to her conversation with Kess, while I watch Hali surreptitiously. She looks happy, lying back in the afternoon sun on her little island.

Not being an active participant in the conversation flowing around me, and more than a little curious, I grab a bottle of water from Kess's cooler and saunter over to the blanket.

"Mind if I join you?" I ask.

"Would it matter if I did?" she answers, without

opening her eyes. Surprise cements my feet in place. She groans and sits up quickly. "Shit, sorry. 'Bitch' is apparently my love language." Her face turns bright red, and she drops her eyes to stare at her lap in horror. "Did I seriously say that out loud?" she whispers to herself before lifting her face back to me. "Sorry, uh, I mean, that was a natural response. Please..." she gestures to the expanse of blanket beside her.

The outburst and her reaction to it amuse me to no end. Part of me likes that I make her nervous, because she makes me nervous, too.

I lie down next to her and take off my jacket, balling it beneath my head as a makeshift pillow. The warmth of the afternoon sun and the subtle scent of her perfume blend into something I haven't experienced much of in the past year...calm.

Still sitting upright, she takes a sip of her juice and reaches for the bag of cookies. Pulling one of the sweet treats out, she holds it between her teeth while she closes the zip-lock on the bag.

Without thinking, I reach up and pull a chunk off, stuffing the chewy chocolate goodness into my mouth before she can complain. She looks down at me, ready to give me shit, and I swallow and grin playfully back.

"Thief." She accuses.

"Hey, you just left it hanging, I figured it was fair game."

"Left it hanging? It was halfway in my mouth," she snorts.

"Po-tay-to, po-tah-to."

She finishes her cookie and wipes the crumbs from her fingers before gesturing to her side of the blanket.

"Do you, uh, mind if I…"

"It's your blanket, you do you."

She lies back again, making sure to leave a good foot of space between us.

Kess lets out a whoop. He must have won the debate because the Deftones' cover of Simple Man starts playing from the speaker we brought with us.

"Has he always been in the band with you?"

I'm surprised she wants to talk, but I go with it.

"We started it together a million and a half years ago."

"Oh, a million and *a half*, huh?" she volleys back.

"That half makes all the difference," I assure her, my lips twitching.

She's quiet for a few breaths.

"What was it like? I mean, were you some wealthy brat who made it big riding your family's money train?"

I burst out laughing, and the conversation by the fire pit pauses for a second before continuing. Hali looks like I bit her and is trying to decide if she should ignore me or punch me again.

"Sorry, I'm not laughing at you, I swear. It's just the

idea of either Kess or I having anybody's money train to ride is hilarious."

"So, what was it like, then?"

"You really want to know?"

"I asked, didn't I?"

I look over at her to gauge her response, but her eyes are closed again as she soaks up the sun.

I tend not to talk much about the early days. First, because anybody that I trust is familiar with the story, and second, because the media doesn't like the truth. They like to take what's real and turn it inside out to make it as salacious as possible. When they're done, the story is so far from how it began that it's laughable.

There's a vibe I get from Hali though. That I can trust her to not run to the nearest tabloid. Not only because it's apparent she doesn't need the money, but because I think she has a good heart under all of her armor. She strikes me as a girl who wouldn't hesitate to push her enemies under the nearest truck, but I've also seen what she'll do to defend somebody she cares about.

"Some of my best childhood memories are of hot summer nights spent cruising around the city. Our stuffy shoebox of an apartment didn't have air conditioning, so Dad would load us into the car, and we'd drive for hours with the radio on and the windows down just to catch a breeze." The memory is bittersweet, its happiness paled slightly by the loss of the one person I loved more than anything. I pause to make sure I can keep my emotions in check.

"What did you guys listen to?" she asks, filling the silence and allowing me a chance to breathe.

"My dad loved classic rock, so I cut my teeth on everything from Lynyrd Skynyrd to Van Halen to Zeppelin. By the time I was ten, he would joke that I sang more than I spoke." My voice cracks ever so slightly.

She pushes up to a sitting position and opens the bag of cookies again. Picking out the biggest one, she seals the bag back up.

"He sounds like a good dad."

I look up at her leaning over me with a chocolate chip cookie in her hand, and her gaze cuts right through me. It's impossible, from the little that I've shared, for anybody to discern if Dad was good or not. But something in her eyes tells me she knows what a good father *isn't*, and that's all the information she needs.

"He was. To both of us."

I take the treat from her and finish it in three bites, while she casually sidesteps my use of the word 'was'.

"You and Kess? Are you guys brothers?" She looks back and forth between us, trying to find a resemblance. Her skeptical grin and the way she wrinkles her nose make my heart skip a beat or two.

"By choice, but not by blood. We both had shitty

mothers. When Dad saved Kess from his, the three of us became a family. We've been inseparable ever since."

"I'm well-versed in shitty parents." A sadness slips over her features, like a cloud passing over the sun. She shakes it off and lies back down. "Tell me more about your dad."

"The year after Kess moved in, Dad found an old Gibson acoustic at a garage sale and bought it for me as a birthday gift. Kess would sit and stare in fascination, his fingers playing air guitar as I strummed the same chords again and again." I turn my head the slightest bit and catch the smile tickling the corners of her mouth. "Dad walked into my room one night after I'd been grinding through the same song for hours, big yellow industrial earplugs jammed in his ears. He jokingly offered Kess a pair, and then spent half an hour leaning against the doorframe watching the two of us."

"Wait, you're admitting you weren't always the rock god you are now? Isn't that the sort of thing you're supposed to keep secret?" She snickers and I can't help but think that sarcasm becomes this girl.

"Rock god, huh? I didn't think you recognized me."

"Oh please." She plucks a handful of grass from beside her and throws it my way. "Modest much?"

"Hey, I can't help it if, by the time we turned sixteen, we'd played a school dance, three birthday parties, and a couple of open mics. We were high school royalty. Chicks dug that shit."

She laughs—a full, rich, sound that stirs something deep inside me.

I grin and continue.

"In all seriousness though, the vocals were what I connected to. Singing has always been my outlet for every emotion that moves me." I clear my throat, not sure why I shared that part of myself with her. "The guitar is something I learned to play. For Kess, it was something that came naturally. When he got his own beat-up acoustic for his birthday, he slept with that guitar for a month, hugging it like a big, stiff teddy bear."

Her laughter is contagious and the two of us enjoy the moment until Kess pipes up from the benches.

"You two okay over there?"

"We're fine," Hali answers. "Ty's telling me all of your secrets."

"Oh, is he, now?" He knows I'm not telling secrets, but he's not one to let an opportunity like this slide. "When you're ready to hear the truth, give me a holler. I'll fill you in about the time Ty got so nervous backstage before a gig, he puked, tripped over his own mic stand, and knocked himself unconscious before we played a note."

I sit up and fire my plastic water bottle at him, which he catches with a chuckle.

Glancing beside me I see Hali trying to keep a straight face.

"Did that really happen?" she asks me.

"No, it did not really happen."

"Yes, it did," Kess singsongs.

"Okay, so it might have happened, but under extenuating circumstances."

She bursts into laughter, and I can't help but smile as she blooms in front of my eyes.

"Some rock god you turned out to be."

"Yeah, yeah." I lay back down, half entertained and half embarrassed. "What about you? I mean I know what you said in group about your parents, but that can't be the whole story."

Her light fades like a dying flower.

"It's not, but I don't want to talk about it." She tries to pull herself out of whatever dark place my question sent her. "Besides, a girl's gotta have a little mystery about her, right? Isn't that what all the advice blogs say?" The look she gives me doesn't plead, but it does ask me to respect the boundaries she's put up around her own life.

Vann leaves her spot on the benches where she's been wrapped in a blanket and discussing everything under the sun with Kess. There's color in her cheeks and an easiness about her that's good to see. Squatting down next to Hali, she leans discreetly, but I can still make out what she says.

"Hals, I have to pee. Are you okay if I leave you here for a few minutes or do you want to come with me?"

"I'm good. I've already punched him once today—if he knows what's good for him, he'll keep his hands to himself." She turns and graces me with an angelic smile that we both know is bullshit.

I bark out a laugh.

"And I will escort you back to civilization," Kess announces, coming to stand at my feet. Offering his hand to Vann with a flourish, he shoots me a quick wink that I hope Hali didn't see.

The two of them disappear through the trees, leaving us to flounder for a minute in the awkwardness of being alone.

"I wanted to apologize about the grocery store," I blurt out and instantly want to kick myself.

"Mmmmhmmmm," is her only answer as she picks at a blade of grass on the blanket.

The silence stretches to awkward lengths, so I push myself to my feet. I can be a pussy, or I can tell her the truth.

Truth wins.

"Look, I have no idea what the hell is going on, but you drive me insane." I rake my fingers through my hair. "Ever since the coffee shop, which by the way you should be apologizing for, someth—"

She jumps to her feet, too.

"Excuse me? *I* should apologize? You're the one who shoved me out of the way and cut the line," her cheeks flush, the calm of our blanket island shattered. "Why the hell would I apologize for that? If anything, you should be apologizing to me. Twice." She starts to stomp away, then reverses direction and comes back, tossing her hair. "Make that *three*times. You were a dick that first day when you barged into my cabin, too."

"Barged? Nobody barged." I laugh like she's lost her mind. "If you hadn't let out that unholy shriek during your tantrum or whatever the hell it was, I wouldn't have come over to investigate."

"Investigate? Is it common practice in your line of work to offer to let random women suck your dick when you *investigate*?"

As soon as she mentions my dick the traitorous bastard gets hard.

Fuck it.

"I've never had any complaints." Lightning quick, I shoot my hand out and fist the front of her sweater, pulling her toward me with enough force that she has to brace her hands against my chest to keep from falling over. My other hand wraps in her thick, silky hair, tugging just hard enough to force her face to tilt to mine, and I crush my lips to hers without another word.

Our tongues find each other, and she takes a sharp breath when she finds mine pierced. Her hands stop trying to push me away, one sliding up my chest and to the back of my neck, while the other snakes down around my waist.

I've kissed a lot of women, that's not something I'll

ever deny. But never in my entire life have I kissed anybody like her.

The electricity pulsing between us could power a small city.

I lift my mouth from hers and trace my forefinger along her jawline. Her eyes open and lock with mine. For a second, all I see is the same need that's coursing through me. Then it's like she suddenly comes to her senses, and shock and fear move in.

She pushes me away and spins on her heel. Snatching up her blanket, she bunches it into a ball and starts striding toward the path.

"Hali, wait," I call, confused as hell.

She doesn't say a word, just breaks into a run and doesn't look back.

CHAPTER TWENTY-TWO

Hali

Sometimes I swear he's watching me, but when I turn to look, he's never there.

It's been three days since the afternoon in the clearing—three days since I ran from the kiss that would've changed everything.

We've had two group therapy sessions and Ty always makes sure to sit as far away from me as possible, which is an impressive feat since Mari has this thing about us sitting in a circle. But somehow, he manages to seem like he's on a whole other planet even when we're in the same room.

I've been plagued by memories masquerading as nightmares since my one on one with Mari, and last night was no exception. Since both of us are dragging ass this morning, Vann and I opt for muffins and coffee from the cafeteria for breakfast. Carrying our bounty outside to the bench by the back door, we sit in sleepy silence and watch the shorebirds hunt as we eat.

"Good morning, ladies," Mari greets us cheerily, coming up the path from the staff quarters.

For a second, a teeny tiny one, the old me wants to rip her face off because I feel like shit, and she looks so damn happy. But the urge passes, and I offer her a flimsy smile instead.

"Are you coming?" She taps the face of her watch and grins at us.

Vann and I groan in unison and follow her inside. We manage to stay awake during group, which is a minor miracle unto itself, and escape back to our cabin as soon as we're dismissed.

"Okay, so who's taking one for the team?" Vann asks, flopping onto the couch once we're inside.

Today is grocery day, and as much as neither of us wants to go, we're running short on a few necessities.

"Let Rochambeau decide—winner goes back to bed, and loser goes to town."

"Dude, I have neither the desire nor the energy to kick you in the crotch until one of us falls down. Veto." She shoots me a double thumbs-down, followed by an immediate thumbs-up. "Bonus points for decision-making creativity, though."

"Not the *South Park* version, spaz. The real game. Rock, Paper, Scissors or whatever you southerners call it." I toss a throw pillow at her.

"Southerners? I'm from Michigan," she laughs.

"Whatever. Sit up so we can do this."

She does, and we do, and I win.

Groaning like a ninety-year-old man with bad knees, Vann drags herself off the couch. She shoves her phone in one pocket and cash in the other, turning back once at the door.

"You suck."

"I know this." I nod sagely in agreement. She sticks her tongue out at me and leaves a peal of laughter in her wake as the door closes behind her.

Not sure what to do with myself now that I'm alone, I wander into the bedroom and stretch out on my unmade bed. We don't have a fan in here, and Vann and I both like the fresh air so we sleep with the windows open a crack. That small opening allows the sound of leaves rustling in the breeze to filter in, and I find myself dozing off.

Full sleep hasn't quite found me when an incredible voice laced with gravel and sin starts singing. I can only pick out a few of the words, but the melody reaches in and wraps itself around my heart.

I roll onto my stomach and push myself to my hands and knees, just high enough to peer over the headboard and out the window behind my bed. The voice is coming from Ty's cabin. At first, I can't see him, so I listen and remember what Vann said that first day about every woman under fifty knowing who Ty was. It makes perfect sense to me now. He might be an arrogant prick, but I'd still let him sing the phone book to me just to hear that voice.

The song stops and before I can duck out of sight, he walks to his window and glances out.

I'm transfixed.

The black, button-down shirt looks like it was thrown on as an afterthought, long sleeves haphazardly rolled up almost to his elbows, and not a single button done up. His torso is tanned and smooth, and holy shit, there are those abs again. His dark hair is wild like he's run his hands through it a dozen times, in three different directions.

Or like somebody else has.

I can't bring myself to look away or stop my eyes from locking with his. And when he smiles at me—a small, secret, 'I caught you' kind of smile—I can't help but return it.

No. This is not how this works. Fucking hell.

Breaking eye contact is almost painful, but I force myself to do it. I slip off my bed and run down the hall to the relative safety of the windowless bathroom.

You hate him, remember? He's the asshole who told you that you have a subpar snatch. The guy that acted like he'd be doing you a favor by letting you give him a blow job. The afternoon at the glade doesn't count. It was probably all bull-shit. Do not—I repeat, do not—be sucked in by a sexy voice and abs for days.

Resolved to get my head out of my ass, I stride back into the bedroom and slam the windows shut. Pulling a thick, full zip hoodie over my tank top and leggings, I dash out of the cabin and straight to the main lodge.

Empty.

Just my luck, the one time I would welcome the company of random people, nobody's around.

"Do you know where everyone is?" I ask the only occupant of the room, a tiny white-haired lady behind the huge desk.

"It's shuttle day today, sweetheart."

"I'm aware." The urge to roll my eyes is strong, but I fight it. "I meant, do you know where everybody *else* is?"

"It was a full shuttle today. They took seven into town, along with Mari and the driver." She stops and double-checks her count with her fingers. "Oh and can't forget the two guests who are leaving this afternoon. I believe they're busy packing." She gives me a cheerful, clueless smile and goes back to her paperwork.

Seven gone, two packing. That leaves Ty and me. Fantastic.

The breeze has become more of an actual wind when I push open the back door and step outside. The sun is warm, but there's definitely a fall chill in the air. Trudging down the path, I'm torn between going back to the cabin and heading to the beach for a walk instead. Before I can make the decision, he calls my name.

"Hali."

Nothing more, nothing less. Just my name.

I try to will myself to ignore him, to keep moving, but I can't resist a quick glance in his direction.

Shirt still unbuttoned, he's standing in the open doorway of his cabin, lounging against the frame like he's posing for a magazine cover. His nonchalance and the memory of our kiss fluster me, so rather than let him see that, I flip him off and continue walking.

"Will you stop, for Christ's sake?" When that doesn't work, he changes his angle of attack. "Unless you're afraid."

Fucker.

"Why the hell would I be afraid?" My feet stop moving of their own accord and I immediately want to chew my tongue off.

"You tell me."

The cocky smirk on his face says he thinks he's won because he got me to react, and the purposeful shift in his stance that opens his shirt wider makes me want to throat-punch him.

"Who the hell do you think you are? Here, let me help you out. You're some rando guy who got lucky in the voice department. Ooooooh, Ty McInnis," I mock, not paying attention to the fact that I've stopped walking away and started walking *toward* him. "Rock god extraordinaire. Stuck out here in the boonies because he can't get his shit together." Three steps away now. "All the money, fame, and women he could ever want, and he still isn't happy. What's the matter, Mommy didn't love you enough? Some long-ago girl-friend get sick of your shit and dump you on your ass?"

Something in my nasty rant must have hit a nerve because before I can blink, he's out the door and gripping my upper arms hard enough to leave marks. He doesn't say a word, just stands there, all tensed muscles and clenched jaw towering over me. Right about now is when a sane person *would* be afraid.

But I've never claimed to be sane.

Curious, angry, frustrated, and turned on, yes. Afraid? Not in the least.

And he knows it.

Tilting my head back for a clear look at his face, I find his gaze waiting for me. I've never been struck by lightning, but I can't imagine that jolt would be any more staggering than the one that happens when my eyes meet his. We stand stock still, staring into each other's abyss, the mist of our ragged breath surrounding us in the cool air until I do the one thing I've been fighting since day one.

Bending at the elbow, my tightly-held arms have just enough reach for my index finger to trace a zigzag pattern from his belly button to the waist of his low-slung jeans. He shivers at my touch, and the sound he makes low in his throat is the sexiest thing I've ever heard. My arms are released from his grip, only to have him reach down and grab my thighs instead. The way he lifts me is quick and unexpected, forcing me to throw my arms around his neck or risk falling over backward. He carries me into his cabin like that and kicks the door shut, before spinning around and slamming me up against it.

CHAPTER TWENTY-THREE

Hali

Slowly, he releases my legs and I slide down his body until both my feet are on the ground, and I find myself pinned between him and the front door.

"This is such a bad idea. I swore this time off was going to be all about me, but I have to have you just once."

He slants his mouth against mine, our tongues seeking each other out. The kiss is rough and deep and intoxicating. His gorgeous lips are firm but not hard, his mouth warm and minty, and the stud in his tongue a massive turn-on.

He pulls back and gives me the strangest look like he's seeing me for the first time. "I don't do girlfriends," he growls thickly, wrapping his hand in my hair and pulling my head back to expose the length of my throat.

"That's good, neither do I."

The brush of his lips as he teases the side of my neck gives me little shivers of pleasure, but when his teeth nip the sensitive skin, it sends an electric shock straight between my legs.

My heavy zip-up hoodie suddenly feels suffocating and cumbersome—a barrier between us that I need to get rid of. One of my hands pulls the zipper all the way down, exposing my skimpy tank top underneath, while the other slips under his shirt. His sharp intake of breath when my cold fingers find the warm skin of his lower back only serves to ratchet up the heat threatening to combust between us.

Waves of pleasure roll through my entire body from whatever it is he's doing to my neck and shoulder. At this point, visible evidence of his feasting on my collarbone is unavoidable and I don't give a shit. Let the gossipy masses talk about the marks I know are going to be there. His lips and teeth and tongue feel so fucking good.

Shifting position slightly, he grasps the front of my tank top with both hands and yanks it down, taking the cups of my plain black bra with it. My breasts spring free, framed by the thin straps of my shirt and bra. His eyes feast hungrily on my exposed flesh, and his strong hands follow, calloused thumbs strumming my pink nipples into rock-hard pebbles.

I'm unable to tear my gaze away from his face, entranced by the need and desire playing across his features while he watches himself play with my tits. When he bends his knees and lowers his head to suck one into his warm, wet mouth, the moan that escapes my throat is involuntary. He uses his teeth to tug on the hardened point, and I have to press my back into the door to keep from collapsing.

"Holy shit, just like that. Use your teeth."

He chuckles darkly with his lips latched onto one nipple and the other pinched between his fingertips, straddling the line between pleasure and pain. As he licks and rolls, bites and sucks, I'm in heaven.

With two last teasing swipes of his tongue, he makes sure the stud piercing it catches purposefully on each jutting peak. Standing up straight, he angles his gaze downward. I let my eyes follow the same path, passing over my exposed tits, and down to my waist. With hitching breaths, I watch as his fingers find the waistband of my leggings and move beneath it to explore. He cups my pussy through my panties and makes an appreciative sound low in his throat.

"You're soaked," he states with a smirk.

"You like to watch," I state with an answering one.

Rather than say anything else, he drops to his knees and tugs my bottoms down until they're around my ankles. Gripping my naked ass cheeks, he adjusts my stance so my pelvis is arched away from the door, then pushes my legs as far apart as my legging-bound ankles will allow. His thumbs trail across the front of my hips until they find their way between the lips of my smooth, bare pussy, and spread them wide to expose the hard bud within.

"I'm not the only one who likes to watch," he says, voice heavy with desire.

He locks his gaze with mine as I stare down at him, entranced, while his tongue snakes out and starts to flick slowly against my clit. I can feel his piercing when he takes long, smooth licks, and watching everything he's doing while he watches me is mind-blowing. My hands find their way to my breasts, and I pinch and roll my own nipples, which makes his tongue move faster.

I'm not a virgin by any means, but I've never experienced anything as hot as Ty eating my pussy like this.

"Oh God." I'm nearly in tears. "That feels incredible."

I let my head fall back and suddenly his mouth is gone, hovering inches from where I desperately need it to be.

"Uh-uh, Rich Girl. The rule is, if you want me to lick your pretty pussy, you're going to watch while I do it. I want to see your face when I make you come."

His words alone are nearly enough to make me do just that, but I dutifully lower my head and meet his eyes.

"Good girl."

He leans forward and starts licking me again, alternating between lapping the flat of his tongue against my clit and sucking it between his lips. Only this time, he also slips two fingers deep inside me, pumping rhythmically against some secret spot that makes me think I might lose my mind if he doesn't stop.

Or if he does.

"Ty, what is tha—" The sensation building at lightning speed within me steals my breath and my words, and I have no control over the way my hips are grinding against him.

"Mmmmmm," he murmurs. "That's it. Fuck my face. I want you to come in my mouth."

His words are muffled but clear enough for me to hear, and I couldn't stuff the genie back in the bottle even if I wanted to. The intense wave of pleasure he's been building in me peaks in a way I've never experienced, and I'm surprised by a gush of wetness between my legs right after he pulls his fingers out.

Oh my God, what just happened?

Embarrassment has me squirming to get away, but he holds my hips in an iron grip and grins wickedly when he lifts his head.

"First time for that, huh? Want to do it again?"

Instead of immediately beginning the rapid downward slide like I'm used to after an orgasm, I'm feeling like I need more. As soon as his fingers slip back inside me, finding that deep, gloriously sensitive spot, he starts tonguing my clit again and I'm lost.

The climb is quick, but this orgasm holds right at its peak for an extended period, and I can't stop coming.

Wave after wave crashes through me, bringing that insane wetness with them, all while I'm trying not to scream with pleasure or pass out.

This time, his mouth doesn't leave my pussy until the last shudder ripples through me and he's licked me clean. Only then does he stand up, his eyes smoldering as he wipes his smirking lips and dripping chin with one hand and reaches into the back pocket of his jeans with the other.

"I've been carrying this around since that first night, trying to fight the urge to use it."

He sticks the condom wrapper between his teeth and undoes his pants, shoving them and his boxers down so his long, thick, and fully hard cock bounces free. His fingers that so expertly play everything from my body to his guitar, stroke his shaft a few times, and a glint of precum shimmers on the head. Tearing open the package, he drops the empty wrapper to the floor before rolling the condom on. Then those same fabulous fucking fingers reach down and spread my lips open again, allowing him to rub his cock slowly back and forth through my wetness.

"I wanted to fuck you so badly, right there in front of the flour and sugar," he whispers with a snicker against my neck while continuing to tease me.

"You told me my pussy wasn't up to par, asshole," I snarl, and turn my head to nip at his earlobe.

"I lied."

He thrusts his hips forward and buries himself to the hilt. I gasp at the size of him, but it quickly becomes a moan as my muscles relax around his dick and I begin to enjoy the feeling of incredible fullness.

"You ready for this, Rich Girl?" he asks, locking eyes with me.

"Fuck me, Ty," I beg, and that's all the encouragement he needs.

Pulling almost all the way out, he drives back in, hard and fast, over and over. His cock fills me completely and each time he pounds into me, it feels like he's going deeper. In this position, standing with my back pressed against the front door and unable to spread my legs fully, his shaft strokes my clit with each thrust and the friction is amazing. When the tip hits the same spot he found with his fingers earlier, my pussy clenches hard in warning. He grips my chin with one hand, making it impossible for me to look away, while his other finds a still rock-hard nipple and twists it between his fingers.

The sensations firing through every inch of me are too much, and the orgasm hits me like a tsunami. He seals his lips to mine, swallowing the scream of ecstasy I'm unable to hold back this time. While he's kissing me, I feel his cock start to throb heavily deep inside me as he finds his own release, coming as hard as I did and ravaging my mouth while he does.

When we're both spent, he pulls back just a bit to

look at me questioningly, our panting breaths mingling, and our bodies still joined.

I'm wrung out.

Drained.

Exhausted.

And I feel the best I've ever felt in my entire life. That was more than sex—it was therapeutic, it was connection, it was incredible. Sweaty, with my tits out, my pants down, and my hair glued to my neck, I gift him a huge, satiated smile. He tilts his head down to rest his forehead against mine before he speaks.

"I have a sneaking suspicion the whole one-off thing just went out the window."

CHAPTER TWENTY-FOUR

Hali

He plants a quick kiss on my lips before heading to the bathroom to dispose of the condom. Stunned by what just happened, it takes me a second to get my brain engaged, and another to be sure I can move away from the support of the door and not melt into a puddle.

When I'm confident my legs will hold me, I remove my shoes, followed by my leggings. Stripping my soaked panties off, I pull my pants back on. They're not the driest things either but I'm not leaving here bottomless, so they'll have to do.

Ty returns just as I'm rejiggering my tank top and bra with one hand while my black panties dangle from the other.

"I like a girl who isn't afraid of going commando," he says with an appreciative grin. Before I can stop him, he snags the underwear from my hand, bunching it up and shoving it into the pocket of his jeans.

"Seriously? Give those back." I fist my hands on my hips and glare at him.

"No way, Rich Girl. You snooze, you lose."

"Stop fucking calling me Rich Girl. You probably have more money than my family does, what with you being Mr. Fancy Rock Star and all. Also, there was no snoozing. I just took the damn things off and then you grabbed them."

My words have zero effect, other than to widen his grin and make him pull my panties out and start twirling them around his index finger. If I was previously sitting at about a seven on the mortification scale, that move has me climbing to a forty-three.

"Are you trying to kill me? Because if you are, there are quicker ways than embarrassing me to death."

Crossing my arms over my chest, I feel a blush heating my cheeks.

"You want your panties back? Come get them."

And like a ten-year-old playing keep-away, he takes off through the living room and down the hall.

I resist the urge to follow him for a full minute and a half. My bare foot taps out a nervous rhythm while I wait for him to come back. It becomes pretty clear he can wait me out, too, so I finally cave.

When I find him, he's already taken matters into his own hands.

Literally.

Leaning back against the headboard, he's lounging on his bed with his shirt still open and jeans and boxer briefs pushed down his thighs. Stroking his dick with one hand, and holding my damp panties in the other, he's sexy as fuck. There's something about a confident man, one who's comfortable in his own skin, that ratchets up the sex appeal.

As if the way the tattoo on his hand undulates slightly with each movement isn't sexy enough.

Or the small, sexy smirk curving that full bottom lip.

Or those gorgeous smoky gray eyes that are dark with both challenge and need.

The wood floor is cool against the soles of my feet as I walk to the end of the bed. When my knees bump the edge of the mattress, I let myself fall forward onto all fours, and prowl my way up his body. The curtain of my hair falls over one shoulder, and the ends tease his naked thigh, raising goosebumps along the tanned skin.

Maintaining eye contact, I run the flat of my tongue from the base of his dick to the tip in one long swipe. He twitches, and when I lick my lips slowly and oh-so deliberately, he thrusts reflexively.

"Looking for somewhere to put that?" I ask.

He nods once.

"Aching for me to wrap my lips around your thick, hard cock and suck until you come down my throat?"

I've never spoken to anybody like this before, but Ty

makes me want to be dirty, and judging by the sparkle in his eyes and the sin in his smirk, he's more than okay with it.

"Yes, please," he growls, and I grin back at him.

He drops my underwear on the bed and uses that hand to twist through my hair, pushing my head lower. With the other, he guides his dick between my parted lips.

I replace his hand with mine, pumping slowly and rhythmically while my tongue swirls and licks. His breathing is ragged, thick with low groans and softly spoken dirty words that ensure my pussy is wet.

Driven to make this as incredible as possible, I take his length in as far as I can. When I feel the smooth head bump against the back of my throat, I swallow around him, creating intense suction and pulling him in just a bit further.

"Holy fuck," he pants in shock, "what the hell was that and can you do it again?"

The surprise and jolt of the added pleasure raise his voice by at least an octave, and I try to stifle my response but it's impossible. The laugh almost chokes me, and I'm forced to pull away. The idea of death by dick just makes me laugh harder, and I topple to the side, like a bridge falling over.

Ty untangles his fingers from my hair, and I look up at him sheepishly, but still unable to stop. I expect him to be like any other guy I've ever been with, angry at the whole 'sex, interrupted' thing and ready to either bail or try to teach me a lesson. Instead, he's watching my uncontrolled laughter with a raised eyebrow.

"I'm sorry," I manage to squeak out through my giggles.

"Glad you find my dick so hilarious."

He's trying to sound pissed off, but the twitches at the corners of his mouth give him away. I roll onto my back, knees bent, and throw one arm over my head, keeping the other at my side. Smiling at the ceiling, I wonder when the shift happened. The one that took me from beaten down, controlled, and viciously unhappy, to this version.

The bed shifts and Ty lifts his hips, tugging his boxers and jeans back into place, but leaving them undone. I can hear his reasoning in my head like he whispered it in my ear—*just in case*—and it widens my smile.

"What are you grinning about now?" The bed dips again and Ty scooches down to lie with his head next to mine, examining the ceiling above us. "Is this like staring at the clouds looking for shapes? Because if it is, we're gonna be here awhile with this flat white paint."

He surprises me again. Past experience tells me this is when he'll say he has to feed his non-existent dog or wash his hair. Any stupid bullshit excuse to get me to leave. But I feel him settle in beside me, the spot between us where our arms touch warm and tingly, both exhilarating and calming.

We stay like that for a few minutes, staring at the blank white space above, each of us painting it with our own hopes and fears.

"I don't want to go home." The words leave my lips before I can pull them back. "I hate myself there. I hate what my father did to me, and I hate what *I* did to everybody else. Going home means going back to that person, because nobody will ever believe I can change. I'm stuck in this skin."

Ty doesn't say a word. But his hand reaches for mine where it rests on the bed between us. He threads our fingers together and for the first time in my life, I feel comforted. That maybe, for once, nobody's judging me by my past.

We've been lost in our own world for the afternoon, but time rudely reminds us of its march forward with voices passing by on the path outside. The window in here is open and under the jeers and laughter, the rustle of paper grocery bags and the crunch of gravel underfoot increase in volume.

"Shuttle's back," Ty says softly.

"Oh, shit! Vann!"

I jump off the bed, letting go of his hand and scrambling for my panties. He doesn't get up, just reaches out a beautifully tattooed arm and snatches them before I can, shoving the ball of silky black material under his ass. I come this close to stamping my foot but resist the urge and plant my hands on my hips instead.

"Gimme."

"Nope. I'm keeping these to play with." The words are said with his usual snark and humor, but something else colors their underside. I'm about to ask him about it, when I hear the faint sound of a window sliding open and look up.

Staring at me wide-eyed from the window above my bed, while I'm framed by the window above Ty's, is my roommate. We do the whole deer-in-headlights thing at each other until Ty, curious about my statue impression, sits up and twists to see what I'm looking at. He waves at Vann with a grin, and I swear, if her eyes get any wider, they're going to fall right out and roll across the floor like runaway grapes.

I turn and bolt, jamming my feet into my shoes.

"Later, Hali. I'll be thinking about you," Ty calls from down the hall, laughing, and even in my frazzled state I know he's going to finish what we started. The memory of him jerking off earlier is permanently etched in my brain and flushes my cheeks pink as I run out the door.

"Stop looking at me like that," I scold. Thinking that helping to put the groceries away might earn me some privacy points was way off base. Since I barreled into our cabin, it's been mostly me putting things away while Vann stares with a mix of awe, surprise, and humor.

"You were just in Ty McInnis' cabin. *In his bedroom.*"

"Yes."

"All afternoon?"

"All afternoon."

She goes quiet, but it only lasts long enough for her to put three cans on a shelf before she's at it again.

"Were you *naked?*" This one she asks with a big smile on her face, so I throw a loaf of bread at her. "Oh, that's a big ten-four on the nakey," she laughs and drops the bread on the counter in favor of clapping her hands with glee.

"Why do you care anyway?" I snap, and her face drops. "I'm sorry, I'm not trying to be a bitch, I swear. I'm honestly surprised you want to know what happened." She accepts my apology and looks at me like I'm nuts.

"How can I *not* want to know? You're my friend so I'd be asking even if it was some Joe Blow rando down the street. But, girl," she grabs my arms and physically shakes me. "Tyler. Draven. McInnis. You were naked with an honest-to-God rock star. One that women all over the world would shank you just to stand next to."

"That's better than their usual reasons for wanting to shank me, I guess."

"No." She slams a jar of peanut butter on the

counter, making me jump. "You need to stop with the self-pity. Right now."

"Self-pity?" I snort, looking at her like she's lost her mind. "Have you met me? I've got no pity for anybody, least of all myself."

"That's horse shit and you know it." She whirls on me, her petite frame seeming much taller in her anger, with her pointer finger jabbing the air in my direction for punctuation. "Every time you make some fucking snide, off-the-cuff remark about people thinking you're shit. Every time you make a comment like you just did about people wanting to shank you. Self-pity. You may not see it that way, but I do. And. Every. Time. It. Happens. He. Wins." Her last statement is accompanied by seven staccato finger jabs, one for each word. "Be better, Hali. Be better than he was, and better than he ever wanted you to be. Be the girl *I've* seen—the one I know you really are."

I don't know if it's Vann's swearing, her finger jabbing, or simply the fact that somebody actually believes in me, but I burst into tears. Me, who didn't cry in front in front of anyone for years because my stupid fucking father would always use it against me when I was younger.

If I'd zipped off my skin like a cheap jumpsuit, I don't think Vann would have been more shocked.

You and me both, girl.

A sobbing, snotty, blubbering mess, I drop to my knees on the kitchen floor and bawl.

"Oh crap. Oh Hali. I'm sorry. Please don't cry."

She squats down in front of me, and I can't speak, so she just wraps her arms around me and holds on tight. We ride out the worst of the tears together, and when I've switched from gut-wrenching sobs to aftermath hiccups, she pulls me up and over to the living room couch.

Once I'm settled, she grabs a box of tissues, a Coke Zero, a bag of salt and vinegar chips, and what has to be three pounds of chocolate. Depositing it all on the coffee table, she disappears into the bedroom and returns with both comforters. One she tosses over me, and the other she wraps around herself before dropping onto the end of the couch and pulling her legs up.

"Okay, go. Give it to me straight, lay it all out there."

She waits patiently, munching on potato chips until I finally find the words.

We sit there for hours, and I tell her the story of a girl who was raised in hell, groomed to bring nothing but pain and fear to everybody around her. A girl who grew up without friends, without kindness, and without a hope of escape—until the day her father died.

Until this place.

While we talk, and the shadows grow long, she tells me her story too. The threads of connection that had

started to appear between us multiply and weave themselves through our words into a bond of friendship. One
I don't think either of us will ever forget.

CHAPTER TWENTY-FIVE

Hali

My head may hurt from crying buckets of tears, and I'm pretty sure I've now proven the existence of junk food hangovers, but when my eyes flutter open long before my alarm goes off, I'm happy. Not the exuberant, jumping up and down, brief spurt of good news happy, but the deep, quiet, feel it in my bones kind.

The kind I was a hundred percent sure would never be mine in this lifetime.

Since for once I'm up earlier than my roommate, I tiptoe out to the kitchen and brew our morning coffee the way she taught me, adding a pinch of cinnamon to the grounds. Being that this is my first solo attempt, I really hope I don't screw it up. Prior to this, my entire hot drink repertoire consisted of being a snotty bitch when going through the drive-thru at Starbucks.

"Did you make coffee?" With a squeal, Vann slides

across the polished wood living room floor in her socks. She's all fluttery and preening like a proud mama bird after I hand her a mug to taste. "Ooooooooh, you did good—this is perfect."

I hide my pleased grin in my own mug, weirdly proud of being able to accomplish such a basic task on my own.

We're getting ready for group when my phone pings with a text message from Mari. Her request to see me for an individual session later this morning dampens my mood slightly. After what happened at the last one, I'm a little concerned about a repeat performance.

On top of that, I'm surprisingly anxious about seeing Ty. What's it going to be like sitting across the circle from him? I know it's just a casual sex thing, but what does that mean exactly? Do we sit on opposite sides and pretend nothing's changed?

I don't know why it's bothering me. The only sex I've ever had has been casual or less. I know how this works.

Sensing my nervousness, Vann tries to make me laugh with awful punny jokes as we leave our cabin. She squeezes a few smiles out of me, but they're shaky to start with, and the closer we get to Ty's cabin the worse they get.

Walking past his door, I'm doing my best to not think about what happened on the other side of it, when it swings open and there he is. Hair still shower-damp, wearing dark jeans, a fitted, long sleeve black Henley, and the most unexpectedly uncertain smile. Like he's been wondering what my reaction would be today, as much as I worried about his.

Vann puts the brakes on and stands in the middle of the path looking back and forth between him and me, a big, goofy grin on her pretty face. Unable to stop my groan at how obvious she is, I roll my eyes and offer Ty an apologetic wince. His half-smile blossoms into a full-fledged grin and my heart squeezes. He joins the two of us and we walk together, me trying to keep my butterflies wrangled the entire time.

Stop it. It was just sex. Really, really, mind-blowing sex, but nothing more than that.

Though she's making every attempt to hide it, I can tell Vann is dying to ask about Kess. She's mentioned him more than once since they met, and each time, her words come faster and a twinkly, happy note creeps into her voice. When she finally caves and asks Ty how his best friend is, he answers with an easy charm and a knowing grin.

I keep my shit in check until we enter the room group is held in and my nervous butterflies turn into bats.

Erissa and Sabrina have saved Ty a seat between them in the circle. Not surprisingly, his ignoring them to sit beside me causes their initial shock at seeing us together to twist into matching ugly sneers.

Trust me, bitches, nobody is more shocked than I am. I'm

*just better at this game than you are, and you'll never be able
to tell my pulse is racing like a greyhound after a rabbit.*

"Slumming, McInnis?" Erissa snipes.

Well, there goes the truce.

Sabrina tosses her hair and sticks her tits out, giving
them a little shake.

"Yeah, Ty. Why don't you come back over here where
you belong? You know we'll make it worth your while."

No actual words leave his lips, but his bark of
laughter bites worse than anything he could've said.

The proximity of Ty's thigh to mine is messing with
my mean girl mojo, stirring up the memory of him on
his bed yesterday, so I opt for a silent smirk and pray
they back off. But no such luck. Off my game or not,
shit's going down.

Since Ty won't take their bait, they shift targets.

"Are you sure you want to back that horse? We know
all about *Harriet*, don't we, Sabrina?" Erissa snickers.

I blanch.

Ty leans a little closer to me.

"Harriet?" he teases quietly.

"Yes, Hali is short for Harriet. Call me that *ever*, and
you'll face a painful, unnatural death," I warn him
through gritted teeth, and feel his chuckle vibrate
through the leg touching mine.

*How the fuck did they find out, though? There is literally
nothing public with that name on it.*

"Daddy was a rapist and probably worse, Mommy

went nuts and tried to kill him, and neither of them wanted their fucked-up kid. You were a very bad girl back in that creepy little town, Harriet. You've done some things that even made us cringe, right?"

Sabrina looks to Erissa for confirmation before continuing.

"All the twisted shit Daddy did to you messed you up bad. We're disappointed, Ty. Thought you had higher standards than a headcase with a carved-up pussy and a shitty attitude."

Christ, these bitches read my file!

There isn't a word in the English language capable of describing what I'm feeling right now. I can't decide which I want more—to feed the stupid twats their own teeth, or for the floor to open up and swallow me whole. Before I have a chance to choose, Vann pipes up.

"You two really are as dumb as you look. Do you realize you pretty much just admitted to a room full of people that you read somebody's confidential files? I mean, that's the only way you could have any of the information you claim to, right? Because you aren't clever enough to come with all that on your own." She shakes her head. "And what the hell is it with you guys and your fascination with dads? For how often you bring other people's up, if anybody's been doing weird shit with their daddies, my vote is for you two creeps."

Silence. Complete and utter hear-a-pin-drop silence.

Then the room erupts into laughter, and none of it is directed at me.

Erissa and Sabrina turn every shade possible between milk white and fire engine red, while I look at Vann with a mix of shock and pride. Never mind the fact that she stood up for me, she totally clapped back at her bullies. It impresses the hell out of me, and I can tell it tickles her too.

"Well played," I say softly.

She grins and shrugs one shoulder.

Mari chooses that moment to join us, and there's an odd little grin playing around her lips. It makes me wonder if she heard any of what happened. If she did, she doesn't let on and group proceeds pretty much the same way it has every day since I got here.

When we're done, Erissa and Sabrina slink out before anybody else, cutting threatening looks at Vann on their way. Discreetly, I ask Ty to walk her back to our cabin on the off chance the idiots get brave and try to cause more shit.

I watch them leave, Vann waving her hands around as she talks.

Squaring my shoulders, I saunter down the hall to Mari's office to face whatever inner darkness she decides to dig up today.

By the time my therapeutic hour is done, all my happy from earlier is marked with bruises and bloody fingerprints. I'm so lost in my own head it takes Ty stepping directly in my path to pull me out of autopilot.

"Hey, I called your name four times. Don't make me use your other one," he teases. But when I lift my face to his all teasing stops. "Come here." Right there in the open he wraps his arms around me and pulls me close.

I resist at first, shoving ineffectually against his chest, but he just holds me tighter, one arm around my lower back and the other around my shoulders.

"You can stop struggling now. I've got you, and I'm not letting go."

His words, and the emotion behind them, split me open. I bury my face in his chest and grip the front of his shirt, my mouth opening in a scream ripped from the depths of childhood terror. The dark fabric absorbs most of the sound, but enough escapes that Vann comes running out of our cabin.

"What's going on?" I hear her voice, thick with concern, but Ty answers for me as my body shakes with anguish.

"She'll be all right. We're going to talk for a bit, and then I'll bring her home, okay?" His hold on me hasn't loosened and I'm grateful for it.

"If you need me, just yell. I'll be right next door." She

runs her hand lightly over my hair once. "Love you, Hals," she whispers and leaves us alone.

Blinded by the volume of my tears, I can't navigate the path, so Ty sweeps my legs out from under me and carries me inside. Crossing to the recliner in the living room, he sits down with me still in his arms and just holds on, resting his stubbled cheek against my hair.

We stay like that, curled together in the big leather chair as long-repressed, unfathomable horrors play out like a movie in my mind, and time ceases to exist.

When Ty finally feels me shift slightly, he slides a gentle hand under my chin and tilts my face to his.

"Tell me."

So, I do.

I tell him what my mother did, and how she's always behaved toward me. I tell him about the beatings, the manipulation, and the mental torture I survived at the hands of my father. I tell him about being raped—the first time by a classmate when I was twelve, and the second a couple of years later as payment for a bad debt owed to one of my father's business partners.

"You know if he was still alive, I'd kill him, right? For every single monstrous thing he did to you."

He says it so matter-of-factly that I believe him.

I lean forward and thank him with a soft kiss before untangling my limbs from his and getting to my feet. There's a strange energy running through my body, and I feel like I need movement to ease it, so I start pacing. Ty stays in his chair, legs splayed, fingers laced together behind his head, and tracks me with eyes bright with fury aimed at a dead man.

"You know, over the years there were so many times I wished I'd never been born. That was his legacy to me." My fingers twist the ends of my hair as I walk the main area of the cabin from end to end, back and forth. "All those things he whispered to me while he broke down the parts he found so distasteful—my curiosity, my empathy, my humanity. When I showed kindness to anything or anyone, he would use whatever was at hand to beat me bloody, but always in places nobody could see. There were so many times I had to sleep on my stomach for days because everything from my lower back to my knees was striped with oozing welts."

Ty's jaw visibly tightens. He doesn't tell me to stop, though. Maybe because he understands this part needs to be said too.

"My mother did nothing to stop any of it. She was never physically violent, but she was also never mentally present. I was left at the mercy of a madman with an agenda."

My throat is filled with the dust of everything I've kept hidden for so long. I stop and get a glass of water from the kitchen, guzzling the whole thing and slamming the empty cup down on the counter.

"For eighteen years I was under the thumb of somebody who was supposed to love me and help me grow into a happy, healthy adult. Instead, he broke my bones and my spirit. Made me unlovable."

My chest heaves because the next part is so hard to admit, but I have to say it out loud.

"I always knew what I was doing was wrong. In order to survive, I had to play by his deranged rules, and adapt or die was the name of the game. I'm a hundred percent sure that if I hadn't, he would have killed me. Beaten me to death in a blind rage. But none of that excuses the things I've done."

I stop pacing and turn to face the man who knows all of my secrets now. Watching the play of emotions across his features, something there makes me think the risk I'm about to take is worth it. That my vulnerability is safe in his hands.

"He made me this way, twisted and torn up, and I let him. I want so badly to be a better person, to be the me that's been hidden inside for so long. But I'm terrified. Without the mask I've worn all these years, the armor I had to develop, I'm open to everything—hurt, pain, crushing defeat..."

I let out a shuddering breath.

"...and you."

CHAPTER TWENTY-SIX

Hali

The words hang in the air between us. My heart is pounding so hard, I swear I can feel it knocking against my ribcage.

Like I'm a frightened cat who'll bolt at the slightest provocation, he slowly lowers his arms and pushes himself to his feet.

One step.

Another.

Keeping his eyes on mine the entire time, until he's standing toe to toe with me.

He brings his hand to my face, cupping my cheek with a hesitancy I would never have expected from him. His palm is warm, and I turn my face into it. I feel the cool silver band glide against my chin as his thumb rubs across my lower lip.

"Is this okay?"

His voice is soft but filled with a sinful promise.

"Yes, please," I answer, mimicking his reply from yesterday.

The hand on my cheek slides to the back of my head and he crushes his mouth to mine. His tongue parts the seam of my lips and delves into the warmth of my mouth, meeting mine in a heated dance. Twining and twisting around each other, the kiss deepens until my legs are trembling.

Both of his hands grasp the front of my oversized plaid shirt and rip, his kiss swallowing my gasp as buttons scatter in every direction. Pushing the shirt from my shoulders and down my arms, his lips move to the spot on my collarbone that makes my toes curl.

"I want you completely naked," he demands, his breath warm against my skin as one hand snakes around my back and undoes the clasp of my bra. I lean forward slightly and shrug it off, a puddle of black lace on the floor at our feet.

Hands around my waist, he easily lifts me onto the small kitchen island and pushes me down flat. The quartz countertop is cold against the bare skin of my back but does nothing to cool the heat pumping through my veins. I fumble with the button on my jeans, and he takes over for me, pulling my pants and underwear off in one shot. The look on his face is pure lust when he grips my ankles and lifts them, kissing the inside of one calf as he places my bare feet on his shoulders.

Now that I'm utterly naked and he's still fully clothed, I'm starting to feel like I'm at a disadvantage. That is, until he grips my hips and slides my ass to the edge of the island. When he drops to his knees, I let mine fall naturally open. My thighs tingle and tighten when he turns his face and covers the ladders of small scars with warm kisses, first on one side and then the other. My toes grip his shirt as they brace and curl against the top of his shoulders. As good as it feels, that's not where I want his mouth, and if he doesn't lick me soon, I might go crazy.

"Patience," he snickers like he can read my mind.

"Fuck patience. I want you to make me come."

This guy makes me bold as hell.

"If that's what you want, you'll have to give me a hand."

"A hand? What do—"

Without changing position, he reaches for one of mine currently braced against the countertop and slides it down the soft skin of my stomach.

Picking up his meaning, I swallow my hesitation and slide two fingers into my wetness, spreading my lips apart and exposing my clit to him.

With an appreciative rumble low in his throat, he lowers his head and laps long, smooth strokes from my opening to the top of my hardened bud, licking the tips of my fingers in the process. When he feels my hips straining to push harder against his mouth, his laps change to flicks and swirls, teasing my clit to insane levels of sensitivity.

My breathing is rapid and shallow, and I know I'm getting close.

So does he.

"Uh-uh. You don't get to come yet. This time you have to wait for me to catch up." He stands, lowering my legs, and I make a move to sit up, but he pushes me back down with a gentle but firm hand on my sternum. He wags a finger at me and shoots me that devilish, dirty grin. Reaching a hand over his head, he grabs the back of his shirt and pulls it up and off. Rolling in into a ball and leaning over to tuck it gently under my head, he props me up. "You're going to need this."

"Oh, am I?" I smirk. He doesn't respond, just straightens up and undoes his belt and jeans, shoving them down and kicking them off.

Holy hell, he's not wearing any underwear, and damn. Damn. Am I drooling? I think I might be drooling.

Standing in front of me totally naked, he's gorgeous.

Broad shoulders, intricate and beautiful tattoos covering each lean, muscular arm from shoulder to hand.

A well-defined torso that narrows to slim hips, the angle of the light playing deliciously off the ridge of each muscle.

The thin trail of dark hair that leads to some pretty impressive manscaping, and his thick, hard cock standing proud against the taut skin of his abdomen. I swear he gets even harder just from me devouring every inch of him with my gaze.

Taking himself in his fist, he strokes the shaft a few times, a bead of moisture appearing at the tip and making my mouth water. He looks me straight in the eyes while smoothly pumping and I know what he's asking.

"I've had an IUD for years. And I'm clean."

His eyes glint.

"So am I. Do you trust me?" he asks.

"Yes," I answer without hesitation.

He lunges for me, quickly sliding me off the island, only to spin me around and bend me over it. Reaching between my legs with one hand, he spreads my pussy wide, and guides the head of his cock to my opening. Instead of driving in hard and fast like yesterday, this time he pushes in slow and deliberate, until he's buried to the hilt. He stays like that for a few seconds, both of us enjoying the sensation of skin on skin.

Then he starts to move.

Making small motions with his hips, the tip stimulates that magic spot deep inside me, making me gasp. As soon as he hears that, he starts to fuck me slowly and thoroughly. With each stroke, my pleasure builds until I'm squirming and shoving back against him, meeting his every thrust. He changes the pace, thrusting faster but no less deep, and my legs start shaking in earnest.

When he squeezes my cheeks and spreads them apart, I have no idea what he's doing until I feel him press a finger against my ass, teasing the opening in small circles. The sensation is something I've never felt before and combined with the friction of his cock deep inside me, I'm racing for my peak faster than I ever have.

"Ty, fuck, oh my God. Don't stop. Please don't stop."

Instead, he speeds up.

"Come with me, Hali."

I feel him start to throb inside me.

"Come all over my cock while I come inside your tight little pussy." His choice of words shoves me right over the edge, sending me into free fall as the most powerful orgasm I've ever had rips through me. He arches over my back as he comes hard and fast, and I press his discarded shirt to my mouth to muffle my shamefully loud moans.

Panting, we stay like that for a few seconds, and he sweeps my hair aside, nipping the delicate skin on the back of my neck. A shiver of an aftershock ripples through me and he slides a hand under my stomach, lifting me to stand with my back against him.

Spent, he gently pulls out and I feel the wetness from both of us on my inner thighs. I turn to face him, and he looks at me with something like awe.

"You're incredible." Pulling me into his arms, he kisses me deeply, erotically, adoringly.

"You're not so bad yourself," I tease when we come

up for air. Planting a quick, smacking kiss on his lips, I look around for my clothes and remember my now buttonless shirt. "I was going to ask if you would mind me having a quick shower to, uh, clean up before I get dressed, but I don't seem to have a shirt to put on," I grin.

"Go. I'll grab you something of mine and meet you there." He smacks my ass as I turn, making me laugh.

The water is cool on my heated skin, and it feels wonderful. I use some of Ty's shampoo and wash my long hair, reveling in his scent.

"Hey, gorgeous, there's a shirt for you here on the counter. My manager just called, and I need to talk to him for a quick sec. Save some hot water for me," I hear him say over the noise of the shower.

"Hurry up, it's lonely in here," I shout back, and hear him laugh as he leaves the room.

I stay under the spray for another ten minutes or so, but when he doesn't return, I decide to get out. Pruney and waterlogged isn't a look I can rock. Using the towel hanging on the back of the door, I dry off and squeeze as much water from my hair as I can. My underwear must still be in the kitchen, so I pull on the faded black T-shirt bearing the Heroin Heartbreak logo, happy to find it's long enough to cover my naked ass.

Ty's voice is raised, coming from the direction of his bedroom. I tiptoe to the kitchen and pull on my panties and jeans. His conversation ends abruptly, and there's a second of silence before I hear something smash.

My stomach clenches in warning, but I force myself down the hall.

He's sitting hunched over on his bed in nothing but black boxer briefs, his elbows on his knees, and fingers buried in his hair. A quick glance around shows me the noise I heard was his phone hitting the wall, presumably after he threw it across the room.

"Ty?"

He doesn't answer.

I cross to him and crouch down in front of him, putting my hands on the outsides of his thighs.

"What's wrong?"

Inhaling deeply, he lifts his face to mine, and I see it swirling in his stormy eyes, chiseled into the set of his lips.

"You're leaving." The words are ash in my mouth.

"Yeah, for Europe," he acknowledges haltingly.

"When?" My voice is so soft, I'm not even sure he can hear me.

"I fly out tomorrow night."

That knocks the wind out of me, but I try not to let it show.

"It's too fast. I mean, I knew I only had twelve days here, but that's stil—"

"You knew?"

The old me wants to rage. To take every little

moment, every shred of connection, and carve it into pieces with the same knife he just jammed into my heart.

But I hold it together.

I push myself to my feet and turn my back to him, busying myself with picking up the pieces of his phone.

"I'll miss you," is all I say, my throat painfully tight with a myriad of emotions.

Being vulnerable is scary as hell for anybody, I'm sure, but for me, it's like stepping off a pier into empty space. He understood that, and he let me do it anyway, knowing anything that happened here would be a memory in a few short days.

I place the smashed phone on the dresser with trembling fingers and walk out of the room.

CHAPTER TWENTY-SEVEN

Ty

I can't just let her walk away.

"You don't have to, you know."

She turns back to face me, her expression unreadable.

"Pardon?"

"You don't have to miss me. There's an alternative."

She doesn't say anything, just shifts her gaze trained out the window.

"Come with me."

The laugh that bubbles from her is dripping with acid and raw, naked pain.

"I think I'll keep my heartbreak on this side of the Atlantic, thanks."

"Damn it, yes, okay, I'm an asshole. I knew about the stupid tour. I expected my manager to be able to buy me more time. I expected to be able to stay longer."

I stand and start pacing, trying to figure out how to make her understand.

"Will you look at me for Christ's sake?" I plead.

When she won't turn her head, I step into her line of sight. Gripping her chin, I forcibly tilt her face to mine, but she keeps her eyes to the side, still refusing to look at me.

"Please, Hali."

Something in my tone finally makes her give in. She slides her gaze to mine, and it almost knocks me on my ass. Her cobalt blue eyes meet my smoky grays, and it's all there. Every piece of her is reflected back at me at that moment, and I know I have to tell her.

"What I *didn't* expect was you."

There's a pause while I screw up my courage to let it all out. But she doesn't give me the chance.

"Fuck you, Ty."

I couldn't be any more stunned if she'd spit in my face.

Pulling away from my grasp, she spins on her heel and beelines for the front door, like she can't get away from me fast enough.

"Wait, what?" I take off after her, managing to slide in front of her before she can reach for the handle. "I just asked you to come with me and you're mad? Tell me what the hell is going on. Please."

"What the hell does somebody like you want with me? I'm such a catch, aren't I? Bad parents, bad attitude, and shitty life skills," she spits. "You've got the world by the ass. Every guy wants to be you and every female over fifteen wants to fuck you."

Her voice rises an octave.

"I can't hear the thoughts in my own head sometimes because they scream at each other and get stuck in the mud of roads rarely traveled." The laugh that escapes her is empty. "You are a literal rock star, yet here you are trying to get through to me. Let me give you a hint—banging your head against this wall isn't worth the time or the effort. My heart died a cold and painfully lonely death long before you came along. There's no resurrecting it now."

Her face is so pale, and she looks so tired and alone that it nearly cracks my heart in two.

"You know you're full of shit, right?" I don't let her answer. "You're so fucking scared of the real you, that even you've forgotten what she looks like. Fear does terrible things. It eats away at our souls and leaves hollow tunnels that lead to nowhere. You pretend not to care that you're alone. You stop crying and you close yourself off to everything and everyone because it's safer that way."

"You have no idea what it was like." The pain lacing her voice is palpable. "If you did, you'd run screaming from me because there is no way you'd believe that a person could withstand all of that and come out the other side sane."

"Why don't you let me decide what I can handle?"

"Look, let me bottom line it here for you. You don't get to do this." Her tone turns icy.

"Do what? What am I doing? Please, enlighten me." My voice is getting rougher as my frustration mounts, flickers of anger biting around the edges.

"You don't get to feed me some bullshit Cinderella story. Make me believe that we can run off together and everything will magically be okay." She swipes at the moisture trailing down her cheeks. "I'm fucking broken, Ty, damaged beyond repair. You don't want me. Not really. What you want is somebody to save. You come bursting in and poke at all my scars, the wounds left behind from years of being treated like a mental and physical punching bag. You see them, all of them, and don't care. They don't scare you. Because you have scars too—deeper and wider than you've let on, but I see them and you know it. As much as you might think you want me to save you, you don't. I know if I go with you, you'll regret asking me to come five minutes after we land, and you'll end up hating me for not refusing in the first place."

I'm speechless in the face of her words, her raw emotion. My heart is pounding, my stomach is churning, and I can't make my vocal cords cooperate.

You write music for a living, you dumb fuck. Find the words. Say something.

But the last word isn't meant to be mine.

"This was only ever supposed to be a quickie, casual thing, so I'll keep it that way. For both our sakes."

She stands on her tiptoes and kisses me softly on the lips.

"Goodbye, Ty."

In one smooth motion, she slips around me and out the door.

And I let her go.

A last lap around the cabin and I'm sure I haven't left anything behind. Nothing tangible, anyway. I jam my smashed phone in my duffel and pull the zipper closed.

I haven't gotten more than an hour of sleep and my head has been splitting since Hali ran from me yesterday. There were so many times in the last twenty-four hours I started to text her then remembered I couldn't. What I needed to tell her should be said face to face anyway. I even made it to her front door once, but the windows were dark, and I couldn't bring myself to knock.

The door to my cabin closes softly behind me. I inhale deeply one last time, hoping to catch a hint of her perfume before I step off the porch, but there's nothing in the air except woodsmoke and pine.

Weighed down with the heavy grief of unresolved

goodbyes all over again, I head up the path to the main lodge where my hired car is waiting for me.

"Looking a little rough this evening, Brother."

My head snaps up at the familiar voice. Kess is on the back lawn, Vann standing next to him.

"What the hell are you doing here?"

He strides over and bear hugs me before taking my bag.

"I figured you might want some company. It's a long fucking trip to Prague." Glancing back at Vann, he gives me a fist bump. "I'll wait for you inside."

Once the doors close behind him, the two of us step onto the porch, and I'm not sure what to say or if I should say anything at all. Thankfully, she speaks first.

"I'm sorry, Ty."

"You have nothing to be sorry for. I'm the one who fucked up." I try for a smile but have a feeling it resembles more of a wince.

"No, you didn't. Timing and circumstance didn't do either of you any favors." She sniffles and her eyes shine. "You're an all right guy, Ty McInnis, and I'm happy I got to meet you." She leans in and gives me a tight hug. "She'll be okay. You both will."

Before I can say anything else, she dashes down the steps and hits the path running.

"Thank you for everything, Mari. I'm sorry that it didn't work out this time." I give her a last squeeze.

Kess blows her a kiss and moves to toss my bag into the trunk of the waiting car, but I stop him, reaching into the side pocket.

"Graduation," is all I say, handing the items to Mari.

"Graduation," she repeats with a nod. "And Ty? Things seem to work out exactly the way they're supposed to." She gives us both a wave and a smile and jogs back up the stairs.

I slip on my sunglasses against the late afternoon light. Even though I knew she wouldn't come to see me off, some small part of me had held out hope.

"Goodbye, Hali," I whisper into the cool breeze and climb into the back of the car.

CHAPTER TWENTY-EIGHT

Hali

My heart squeezes painfully, leaving behind a horrible, empty, dull ache. The split second of excitement his suggestion to go with him sparks quickly turns to mind-numbing fear.

Everything that my father ever whispered in my ear, all the promises that nobody would ever give a shit about me, that I was worthless, come rushing back. My mind has no idea how to process what the gorgeous, talented man in front of me is asking. All I know is I'm not equipped to deal with it, and it terrifies me. So, I do the only thing I can.

I destroy it all.

My harsh, caustic words set every soft thing blooming between Ty and me ablaze, until all that's left is the ashy taste in my mouth and the look on his face.

Shock, anger, denial—all of them play across his

features. But the ones that will stick with me forever, the ones permanently seared into my heart are longing, grief, and something unfamiliar, something I'm too afraid to name.

I turn and flee the cabin, racing for the privacy of the beach. The weather has shifted again, and the Heroin Heartbreak T-shirt does little to protect me from the chill of the incoming storm. My feet scrabble for purchase as I slip and slide over the jetty while the wind tries its hardest to blow me off course, but I have to know. When I reach the tabletop rock, I scrape my hands bloody searching everywhere around it for Ty's secret stash of colored stones.

They're gone.

I wanted them to be there, a tactile reminder of him and a talisman to have near me when things get too dark, too scary, too real.

My hair clings to my face and neck, drenched by tears and the spray coming off the water. Shoving the dripping mess out of my eyes, I drag myself onto the flat surface and mourn everything I've lost or never even had.

The sound of my name being called filters through the rain and suddenly my only friend is climbing up beside me. The two of us sit for God knows how long, holding tight to each other's hand while the wind tangles our hair and steals the sobs from my lips.

"Hals, we should go back. Your lips are blue, and I can't feel my fingers."

The cold didn't register until she mentioned it, but now my teeth won't stop chattering. We half carry, half drag each other back to our cabin through the gathering dusk, and once inside, I stand in the kitchen, soaked and freezing. Vann flicks the switch to ignite the gas fireplace and then disappears down the hall for a few seconds. She returns carrying a bundle of clothing.

"You need to get those wet clothes off or you're going to get sick." When I don't move, she comes to stand in front of me. "Arms up."

I do as I'm told, and she strips the T-shirt over my head and hands me my pajamas. Once we're both changed, she shoves our wet things into the dryer in our tiny laundry room.

She herds me toward the bedroom, and when she senses my resistance, assures me that the windows and blinds are all closed.

I climb into my bed, wrapping the comforter around myself like a multicolored cocoon, and huddle there miserably.

"Tell me what happened."

The smell of peppermint tea fills my nostrils as she sets a piping hot mug on my nightstand. Plopping down on the end of my bed, she crosses her legs and waits, patiently blowing on her own tea.

When I'm finally ready to talk she lets me ramble

about my father, my half-sister, and the mess I made back in Folkestone. I tell her about the abuse I endured and the hate I dished out. She listens to it all without a flicker of judgment.

But the one thing I can't talk about, the one thing I need to keep all to myself right now, is Ty.

"I mark the passage of my life with milestones of pain. Other people have birthdays and parties and proms. I have bruises and scars and things that live in dark corners." I bite my lip to keep from sobbing. "I know it sounds stupid, but the parts of me that he lit up, and the moments when I felt whole...I'm so scared that they'll disappear if I examine them too hard." My chest hurts thinking about how he made me feel. "I need to hold on to them as long as I can."

"It doesn't sound stupid at all." She reaches for my hand and gives it a tight squeeze. "When you're ready, you'll realize you put those pieces back together all on your own. He just helped you celebrate them."

As exhausted as we both are, we stay up most of the night, drinking tea, talking, and watching silly videos of people on the internet. When neither one of us can keep our eyes open, Vann stumbles over to her bed and face-plants onto it, sound asleep and snoring within minutes.

It takes me a little longer, but when sleep does grace me with her presence, I dream of Ty's grit-on-silk voice singing a haunting tune of loss and regret.

THREE WEEKS LATER

light
lightly sw

CHAPTER TWENTY-NINE

Ty

I *fucking hate hotel rooms.*

Impersonal, boring, and filthy at a microscopic level if you can believe any of the forensic dramas on television.

I press the call button for the private elevator to my suite a few more times in my impatience, like doing it more than once will make it show up faster. When the black mirrored door finally swishes open, I hammer the only button on the brushed aluminum panel a few times, too.

Tonight's show was rougher than usual and all I want to do is take a long, excruciatingly hot shower. As soon as I step out into the penthouse, I unzip my boots and kick them off in different directions. My shirt gets tossed on the glass-topped dining table, my black leather pants get peeled off and thrown on the end of the king-size bed, and I walk into the bathroom naked and sticky with sweat.

Stepping into the shower that's large enough for at least twelve people, I face the spray and press my palms against the wall in front of me. I roll my shoulders a few times then duck my head to let the hot water sluice down my neck and back. The temperature helps loosen the muscle I cranked on stage tonight but does very little to improve my mood.

Everything has felt strange since I left the States. From the second the plane took off for Prague, I constantly feel as though I'm forgetting something. I even had my assistant call our previous hotels last week to make sure I hadn't left anything behind. She likely thinks I'm crazy now, but if I said I give a shit, I'd be lying.

My heart just isn't in this tour, and even if the fans and the press keep raving about how great the shows are, I know they're not what they could be. I'm just thankful it's almost over. Tonight was the second of three back-to-back shows in London—come Monday morning, we head home to Los Angeles, though I don't know how long I'll stay. I've been thinking about a holiday somewhere as far from civilization as possible. Kess is down with the idea of coming with me, his only stipulation being that 'isolated' still has wi-fi.

Once I'm out of the shower, I tug on a pair of light gray sweats and wander shirtless into the living area.

Just as I'm about to flick on the television in search of distraction, there's a click as a keycard is used and the suite's main door opens a crack. I have a perfect line of sight from my seat on the black leather L-shaped couch as a chunk of blond hair and a single blue-white eye appear in the gap.

"Are you decent?" Kess whisper shouts.

"Am I ever?"

"Not that I'm aware of."

He pushes the door all the way open and backs into the room, dragging a fully laden room service cart with him. Turning to face me, his eyebrows shoot up.

"Did you try to boil yourself?" he asks.

"Shut up. I pulled something in my shoulder on stage and I wanted the heat."

"Mmmmhmmm. Whatever you say, Lobster Boy." Dismissing my appearance, he waves a hand grandly over the cart. "I come bearing gifts."

He parks his spoils next to the dining table and beckons me to join him. I shake my head.

"Brother, you can't survive on melancholy and what-its forever." He lifts one of the silver lids and uses it to waft the scent of the pasta it covered my way. "Look, I brought you carbs. Chicks swear by them when they're all sad and shit, so I figured it was worth a try."

Knowing he won't stop until he gets his way, I join him at the table.

"I'm fine. Really."

"Okay, so you're fine. You still need to eat, even if you're a morose motherfucker these days."

"Steady mentioned something about an after-party in your suite tonight. Lots of women with questionable morals in attendance. So, what the hell are you doing here eating pasta with me?" I ask and arch an eyebrow at him.

"Point taken," he laughs, handing me a plate and taking his to the other side of the table.

"So, today's the day, huh?" He asks, forking a twirl of Bolognese-covered noodles into his mouth.

"Today's the day. Or yesterday was the day? It's tomorrow here for them, and I think it's still yesterday there for us?"

"Put a lot of thought into this, have you?" he chuckles and shakes his head.

"The damn time difference always screws me up," I growl and give up trying to figure it out.

By the time we finish eating, it's almost three o'clock in the morning. We load the dirty dishes back onto the cart and Kess starts pushing it toward the door when he catches sight of the elevator in its alcove off to the side.

"What is *that*?" he demands, with a sharp intake of breath.

"That's called an elevator. E-l-e-v—"

"I know how to spell it, thanks. But why is yours private when the rest of us peasants have to use the same one everybody else does?" He plants his hands on his hips and taps his foot comically.

"At least you've got your own giant shower this time," I point out.

"Yeah, but you've got an *elevator...*"

"Goodnight, Kess." Laughing, I shove him into the hall and close the door.

For the first thirty seconds or so, when I'm still floating in blurry half-sleep, everything is right with my world. Nothing hurts, nothing's missing, and nobody's gone.

Then I open my eyes and it all comes rushing back.

I let the weight of it settle into my chest and force myself out of bed, both shoulders stiff and tight. Yawning like a bear, I paw through the closet for a hoodie, and just like they've done every one of the past twenty-two days, my fingers linger for a few seconds on the plaid, button-less shirt that still holds a hint of her scent. Kess is the only one who knows I brought it with me after she left it behind, and what those ten short days on the Sound meant to me.

Rubbing my left shoulder, I pop a pod into the machine and make myself a coffee before picking up my guitar and carrying both to the couch.

One more show.

My fingers pluck out the opening chords of something I started writing after my dad died. It got held up for a little while, my creativity corked by loss and grief, and languished as only a possibility.

Until that night.

When she ran, it was like the floodgates opened and I was almost washed away by the emotional tidal wave. I poured everything into this song and finished it in the darkest hour before dawn. Wrung out and exhausted, I hiked down to the jetty and sat and watched the stars twinkle out one by one.

As the sun came up and the shorebirds arrived for their breakfast, I made my way back to my bed and slept until it was time for me to go.

A sharp rap on the door and the click of the lock pull me out of the memory, and I look up as the guys stumble in. Normally, Kess would be the ringleader, the purveyor of all things sinful and fun, but he's the only one who looks like he actually got any sleep last night. This whole leg of the tour has been like that, and I'm not sure if it's because he's worried about me going off the deep end or if he's got something else on his mind.

He and Steady join me on the L-shaped couch, while Logan and Noah drop into the club chairs across from us.

"You realize that song is incredible, right?" Logan, our drummer, puts his feet up on the coffee table and crosses his ankles.

Steady reaches out and pushes his legs down.

"Were you born in a fucking barn? This is a meeting, keep your feet off the damn table."

Logan grins and flips him off, and Steady returns both gestures.

"This is a meeting?" My bullshit meter is going off like crazy. I'm definitely missing something, and I look around suspiciously at the faces of my bandmates and our manager.

"Yeah, sorry about the ambush, but tonight's the last show of the whole tour, not just this leg. We were thinking we should end with a bang." Noah is the youngest of us, joining Heroin Heartbreak after our original bassist decided marriage and a mortgage were more his style. At twenty-one, I'm pretty sure he thinks everything should end with a bang.

"I already regret asking this, but what do you have in mind?" All kinds of ridiculous scenarios flash through my head, most of them involving flames or spinning drum kits or the cops.

They're all silent until Steady finally has the balls to spit it out.

"They want to play the song."

My answer is immediate and adamant.

"No."

Setting my guitar down, I get up and walk out of the room.

"Come on, man, it's the perfect thing to close the

show with," Logan says to my retreating back.

"It's not a bad idea, Ty," Steady chimes in. "It really is a fantastic song. Hits you right in the junk."

Kess snorts.

"That's *feels*, Old Man. Hits you right in the feels."

"Call me Old Man again, Kessworth, and I'll hit *you* right in the feels."

That sets all of them off and their raucous laughter reverberates through the suite.

I ignore it and throw myself on the bed, too tired of the bullshit to argue. They've been after me to add the song to the setlist since they first heard me play it in a Prague hotel room, but every time they ask, I refuse.

Steady seems to clue in that their little musical intervention did nothing to further their cause, so he plows them all out of the suite—all except Kess. He saunters into the bedroom and stretches out on the chaise.

"You know I wouldn't dream of trying to tell you what to do, Brother, and I've always got your back."

He steeples his fingers over his chest.

"You might as well say what's on your mind because there sure as hell was a giant neon 'but' at the end of that statement." I push myself up on my elbows and glare at him.

"Buuuuuuuut," he says with a grin before getting serious again. "It's time."

"Time for what? Time to make a fool out of myself? Time to rip my guts out on stage in front of twenty thousand people?" I half ask, half shout, incredulous that I'm having to have this conversation with him, of all people.

"That last part could get a bit messy, but yeah, pretty much." He shrugs.

"Why?" I groan. "Give me one solid reason why we should add the song."

"Because it's driving you crazy. You've been dragging it around with you like a boat anchor for three weeks, Brother. You wrote it for a reason—"

"Yeah, I did." The frustration threatens to overwhelm me. "I wrote it for me, Kess, *for me*. I wrote it to try to make sense of everything in my head, to try to see things clearly for the first time in a long time. I wrote it to grieve." I sit up and rub my temples, the beginning of a headache blooming behind my eyes. "I wrote it to say goodbye."

"Then let's grieve, let's say goodbye. That song is epic, I shit you not. Even Steady had goosebumps when you played it. I know that for a fact. Rolled up his sleeve and stuck his arm right in my face. Told me all the little hairs standing on end meant your song was a unicorn."

I can't help the grin that twitches my lips at the image of Steady showing off his goosies.

"I've never lied to you, Brother. Not even when it would have saved you some pain if I had." He sits up and meets my eyes. "There's some powerful emotion woven into your words. Let's get up on that stage tonight in front of all those screaming fans and blow their fucking faces off. Do it for your dad, do it for yourself," he pauses, "do it for her."

As much as I'd love to tell him he's wrong, I know he's not. I've been holding it so close, not wanting to share my loss, my heart, that it's started to fester. It's time to let it go.

With a resigned sigh, I get up and shoo him out of the bedroom.

"Go tell them to get their asses in gear. I'll change and meet you downstairs in five to rehearse. If we're doing this tonight, nobody's going to fuck it up."

Hali

The breeze off the water has gotten colder over the past three weeks, but I couldn't leave without visiting the jetty one last time. The tabletop rock is still the place I come to find my peace when the darkness starts to creep back in. The midday sun is warm on my skin, and the whispers of the water on the shoreline are filled with hope for the future.

It doesn't seem like it's been just over four weeks since my mother dumped me on The Overlook's doorstep. Part of me feels like I only just arrived, while a deeper, more intuitive part feels like my missing pieces were always here, waiting for me to come and find them.

The work I've done here has been tough. I think it would have been regardless, but after Ty left, it was absolutely brutal for a while. Some of the darkest nights of my life were spent in the cabin, huddled in misery and drowning in tears. Those were the nights I wanted to quit when I would have done anything to make the nightmares stop. Vann was always there when I'd wake up in a cold sweat, screaming about a madman and all the ways he tried to turn me inside out.

Mari has become somebody else I trust implicitly. She stuck by me, pushing when I wanted nothing more than to stay stuck, and celebrating every success no matter how small. She helped me see that I'm not what my father tried to make me—that I'm more than merely a puppet of his creation.

Standing, I close my eyes and make a wish, sending it out in the Universe with a kiss before making my way to the path.

I took my bags up to the main lodge earlier, so there's nothing left to do except say goodbye to Mari. Slipping in the back doors, I head down the hall to suite 107 for the last time.

"Hali." Mari smiles around my name when she opens her office door and ushers me inside. "How are you feeling about going home today?"

We sit down and each of us grabs a candy from the dish on the low coffee table between us.

"Honestly, not great," I sigh. "I don't know if Folkestone can ever really be home again. I don't know if I want it to be. A huge part of me has always felt trapped there, but maybe things will be different now that I'm different."

"You're doing so well and I'm so proud of you. Don't ever let anybody try to tell you that you haven't worked your butt off." A shadow shifts briefly through her eyes, and I know exactly what she's referring to.

Mari thought having my mother come to one of the visitor's days and participate in a therapy session would be good for both of us. Start trying to build some bridges and set up a support system. Eleanor never showed up. She sent her regrets all the way from Sardinia, where she was too busy cozying up to her new—and much younger—boyfriend to go out of her way for me. It would have been nice if she declined *before* we were supposed to be in the session, but hey, that's Eleanor. I never expected her to come, but it really chapped Mari's ass that she couldn't be bothered. I've forgiven my mother for not being able to save either one of us from my father, but we'll never have a real relationship, and I'm okay with that.

"I'm learning to accept that I can't change the past—that I can only move forward. There's still more work for me to do, but I'm not who I used to be. For the first time, I feel like my own person."

"I love hearing that." She beams like a proud mom. "When things get hard—because you know they will sometimes—always remember the shattered vase. You could spend forever trying to rebuild it with tape and glue and edges that don't quite fit together. You may end up with something that looks like a vase again, but it will never be solid, never be strong." She reaches forward and gives my hand a quick squeeze. "Instead, keep using those same pieces to create a beautiful, colorful mosaic and embrace the stronger, more resilient, and incredibly capable woman you're becoming."

"You're bound and determined to make me cry before I leave, aren't you?" My vision blurs with tears but I blink them back and grin.

"You've come a long way from the angry girl who stepped out of that car a month ago. I think that deserves a few happy tears."

We stand and she hugs me. I squeeze her back tightly, grateful to her for never giving up on me.

"Thank you so much, Mari. For everything."

"This place is always here for you, I'm always here for you, just a phone call away." She clears her throat of her own unshed tears. "Okay, you're all packed? You've double-checked to make sure you have everything?"

"My bags are on the porch, and all of my flight information is on my phone." My mother transferred a chunk of money to my bank account and left me to my own devices. I guess throwing money at things is easier than actually having to deal with them yourself.

She links her arm with mine and we walk to the front door together.

"Tell me something you're looking forward to when you get home. What's the first thing you want to do?"

"I want to see my sister," I answer without hesitation.

There's a sentence I never thought I'd say.

As part of the program here, I had to choose one person to make amends with. The list of people I owe apologies to is long, but the one that stood out the most was my half-sister. Mari initiated the contact and the reason for it, and to my complete shock, Stella agreed to speak with me.

That first phone call was awful—awkward, messy, painful, and full of anger on both sides. But she shocked me again when she asked if we could talk again after she had a few days to process everything.

We've spoken three more times over the past couple of weeks. While I'm not expecting any miracles and whether or not she can forgive my past behavior remains to be seen, we made a plan to meet up in person when I get home.

"I'm thrilled for you, Hali, I really am."

The driver is standing next to the hired car, ready to take my bags when we emerge from the building. I remember how out of place they looked when they were unloaded, and how much their bright hue annoyed me. Now, they just look pink.

Mari leans in for one last hug before reaching into her back pocket.

"There's one more thing." She presses a tiny box and

a sealed envelope into my hands. "These are for you. From Ty."

A warmth flows through me at the mention of his name, threaded through with longing.

My soul misses him every day—the electricity between us, our banter, the way he touched every part of me. But I know my decision was the right one. There was no way I could have left with him to fly halfway across the world on a whim. On top of my needing to figure out how to thrive on my own, the idea of me as a groupie is a comical one. I still lick my cookies some-times so I don't have to share, and I would have had to share him with everybody from his bandmates to his fans.

"He gave these to me before he left, and asked me to pass them on to you the day you completed the program. Your graduation day."

The driver has my bags loaded and the rear passenger car stands open. I squeeze Mari again, not fully trusting my words at the moment, and climb into the backseat clutching the box and the envelope to my chest.

As we pull out onto the road that will take us to the airport, I suck in a deep breath and decide to open the plain white box first. My fingers work the lid off, and the polished scarlet stone nestled inside makes me chuckle through the tears now spilling freely down my cheeks.

This is the one I wanted when I went looking that day. The one that will always remind me of him.

Of course, he knew that.

Because he knew me.

Holding the stone tightly in one hand, I carefully open the envelope and pull out a single sheet of paper folded in thirds.

Happy Graduation Day! I'm so proud of you for seeing it through and doing what was right for you.

You never needed saving—you had it in you to do it on your own all along.

You were right when you said I have scars. One of the deepest, a parting gift from my own mother. I swore I'd never let another woman get that close to me again, and I've been completely successful at keeping that pledge to myself.

Until I met you.

There are no coincidences. Everything about the first verse of you and I happened exactly as it was supposed to.

Take care of yourself, Hali.

Love,

Ty

The words shimmer and blur and I close my eyes against the tears.

The tour started right after he left, and one of the tabloid TV shows Vann is addicted to ran a feature on Heroin Heartbreak and the personal lives of the band members. She tried to change the channel when it came on, but I wouldn't let her. Ty's segment was by far the shortest, and the most barren of detail, even though he's the lead singer. When they ran a small clip of the band from one of the Prague shows, I watched with my heart in my throat, greedy for a glimpse of him even though it hurt more than I ever thought it could.

Everything that happened between us happened so incredibly fast, but for me at least, every bit of it was real. And even though I had to let him go, he'll always have part of my heart.

The driver pulls up in front of the departure area and parks with his hazards on. I don't wait for him to come around and open my door, and climb out on my own instead. He unloads my bags for me, placing them neatly on the curb. I thank him, tip him, and head into the terminal, grinning to myself when both suitcases roll smoothly along, not smashing into my ankles once.

Before I get more than five steps inside the doors, my phone starts playing 'Dynamite'. Pulling it out of my pocket, Vann's face smiles up at me from the caller ID.

"Did you really need to change the ringtone, too?" I laugh when I answer.

She went home to Michigan three days ago and insisted on triple checking all of her contact information on my phone before she left.

"Where are you?" she practically yells, out of breath.

"At the airport. Why?" My stomach flutters uneasily.

"Duh. I mean where are you at the airport?"

"I just walked in the main doors. What's the matter with yo—"

Before I can finish my sentence, she shrieks and I hear it in stereo.

What the hell?

The call disconnects and I look around just in time to see her racing toward me, black hair flying out behind her, wearing hot pink sweats and a big grin.

"Vann! What are you doing here?"

"Come on, we have to hurry or we'll miss it." She rips the handle of one of my bags from my hand, pulling it along with her own. "Seriously, Hali, I love you to bits but if you don't move your ass..."

CHAPTER THIRTY-ONE

Hali

This is my crossroads.

"Are you kidding me?" I ask, floored by her suggestion.

"Nope. I made the executive decision that we are going to catch Heroin Heartbreak's last London show." Her smile falters in the face of my silence.

My emotions are short-circuiting while I try to process everything she's said.

England.

Concert.

Ty.

I can go home to Folkestone as I'd planned.

Or I can fly thousands of miles to a different country with my best friend, to catch a glimpse of a relative stranger who made me feel things I never thought were possible.

What the fuck do I do?

"Hals?" Vann asks, waiting for my decision.

Everything about her seems so much lighter than when we first met. Or maybe it's me that's lighter. All I know is that after she clapped back at Erissa and Sabrina when she stood up for me, they stopped bothering her. She was more confident, less anxious, and truly happy.

And now she wants to do this for me.

I know in my heart which path is the right one.

"Okay, let's go to London," I agree with a huge grin, and she shrieks again.

Now that we're actually here, I'm seriously questioning our sanity. For the last thirty minutes of our flight, every possible thing that could go wrong with this impromptu trip ran through my mind. And now my feet won't let me move from where I'm standing next to the baggage carousel.

This is the stupidest thing I've ever done, and that's saying something. For all I know, Ty forgot about me two minutes after he got on the plane. He's had plenty of time to stick his dick in a multitude of willing females. I'm nobody. Just some random chick he spent ten days in the woods with.

"Are you all right?" Vann peers at me in concern. "You like you're either going to pass out or shit yourself."

"To be honest, it could go either way right now." My

hands are ice cold and won't stop clenching and unclenching.

"Do you trust me?"

"I just flew across an ocean on five minutes' notice with you…what do you think?" I snap at her, even though we both know I don't mean to.

"Then believe I'd never do anything to hurt you."

"Where are we going? Do we have a car? A place to stay?" My words are coming sharper and faster, firing at her like bullets. "Do we even have *tickets*?"

"Let's get out of the terminal, okay? I hired us a car." She checks her phone. "It should be waiting for us."

Once we get outside into the cold evening air, I suck in a few deep breaths and feel my lungs start to behave normally again.

"Over there." Vann points to a rotund uniformed driver holding a sign in front of a glossy, black Mercedes S-Class.

"'Vann Hali'? Really?" I snicker.

"Hey, they asked who the car was for when I booked it. I thought it might make you laugh, and it did. So there." She sticks her tongue out at me.

When we pull up to the hotel nearly an hour later, I'm stunned. I had no idea what I expected, but it damn sure wasn't the sky-high, gleaming, architectural wonder in front of us.

"Uh, Vann? Are you sure you gave the driver the correct address?"

She grabs my arm and tugs me into the lobby filled with laughter and music from the attached bar. Our bags materialize on a luggage cart pushed by a handsome bellboy while Vann gets us checked in.

I follow her to the elevators, open-mouthed, in awe of how beautiful and perfect everything is, and I'm speechless all the way up to the forty-first floor.

Opening the door to our room, Vann discreetly tips the bellboy and I get my first look at where we're sleeping tonight.

"Holy shit." Overwhelmed and exhausted, I flop onto the bed and lie there, stretched out like a starfish. "This is ridiculous, you know," I address the ceiling. "The flights, the car, this hotel room. I'm paying you back for all of it."

Vann makes a dismissive noise from where she's digging through her suitcase.

"It was cheaper than you think," she answers critically. She comes over to the bed and yanks on my ankle, tossing a phone charger with a weird-looking plug on it next to my head. "The concert starts in half an hour. We're going to miss the first bit, but I don't want to miss too much, so get up."

Once my phone is plugged in, I have a minor freak out about what to wear. I rush over to my luggage and unzip the large bag. Three seconds away from bursting into tears at the sight of sweatpants and my stupid fucking Woodington uniform skirt, a sparkle catches my eye.

Thank you, angry packing Gods.

The shimmery silver camisole I shoved randomly in my bag a month ago is perfect. I grab it, and a pair of low-rise, tight black jeans I didn't wear once the whole time I was in Washington, along with a clean black bra and panties. Digging through my other bag, I find a pair of heeled black leather boots and my toiletries.

I'm sitting cross-legged on the bed applying liquid liner with the aid of a handheld mirror when Vann emerges from the bathroom.

"You look incredible," we exclaim simultaneously before bursting into laughter.

Her long hair is twisted up into space buns, and the only makeup gracing her pretty face is black mascara and a pop of deep, ruby-red lipstick. Dressed in dark jeans as well, she's paired hers with a black cropped T-shirt, and platform Docs.

"Are you almost ready?" She does a pocket check to make sure she's got everything she needs.

"Yep." I slick on my favorite raspberry gloss. "Just let me grab my ID and some cash." I fish through my purse and pull out my passport. "Hey, how did you get this by the way?" I wave the little booklet at her.

"Eleanor came through for something." She cackles. "Mari called her, and she called your housekeeper and had her courier it to me. So, I guess your housekeeper actually came through."

"Mari knew? How long have you had this planned?" Once again I'm in shock.

"Don't you worry about that." She moves to stand in front of me and tucks my pin-straight hair smoothly behind my ears. "You look beautiful."

"Wait, I need one more thing." Reaching back into my purse, my fingers find the small, red stone. I shove it in my pocket . "Okay, I'm good."

"This is going to be amazing," she assures me and pulls the door closed behind us.

T he show is in full swing when we walk into the venue nine minutes later. From the sounds of things, the crowd is eating it up. Twenty thousand screaming people must mean you're doing something right.

"You have the tickets, right? Where are we sitting?" I yell over the din.

She just grins cheekily, reaches into her back pocket, and slips a lanyard over my head.

"What the hell?" I turn the laminated rectangle so I can read it. The band name and latest album cover stare back at me, VIP written in bold, block letters across the bottom. "How—" My stomach is swarming with butter-flies, all of them flapping their delicate wings at the same time.

Vann doesn't say a word. She hangs her own lanyard around her neck and grabs my hand, pulling me over to a burly man in a 'Security' shirt. He takes note of our passes and nods to an equally hulking man who escorts us to the backstage area. Speaking into his headset, he gives us a little wave and turns to go back to his post.

"Wait." I reach for his bicep that's as thick as one of my legs, concerned he's abandoning us.

He flicks his chin to something behind me and walks away.

Turning in the direction he gestured, I see a decent-looking middle-aged man of average height and weight approaching us. He sticks out a hand in greeting, leaning in to introduce himself.

"I'm Nick Steadman. You can call me Steady." After shaking both our hands, he beckons for us to follow him.

He leads us through a warren of dressing rooms and waiting areas. There's even a bar back here. A group of women jeer and joke with staff and each other as we approach, but fall silent when we walk by, shooting icy glares our way.

We walk for another minute or two and Steady points to a set of stairs ahead. The music here is so loud, it feels like the drums are going to alter the rhythm of my heart. Vann starts the climb, and I trail behind her with Steady bringing up the rear.

Once we get to the top, the space opens up. Overwhelmed with lights and sound and heat, I have to remind myself to breathe. Vann looks back over her shoulder and sees my hesitation so she grabs my hand and holds on for dear life.

The joy plastered all over my best friend's face makes my heart happy. I don't think she's known a whole lot of good in her life, and I'm honored to be part of this moment with her. Never in my life have I seen anybody as ecstatic, as *alive*, as she is, drenched in moving colors, wailing guitar riffs, and vocals that sound like sin.

Steady clears a path for us and we work our way up to the edge of the stage.

And it hits me.

It's Ty on stage. It's *his* voice that's crawling under my skin and making it almost impossible to keep my feet still. It's Kess that has the small group of guys next to us playing air guitar like their lives depend on it.

For some reason, my brain knew we were coming to see Heroin Heartbreak, but it refused to make the connection that Ty and Kess *are* Heroin Heartbreak.

We dance and laugh like lunatics for close to an hour, and every movement that he makes, every note that he sings, lights up something inside me that's only ever known shadow.

I'm so mesmerized and lost in the emotion, that it

takes me a second to realize they've stripped the music down to a simple drum beat while Ty addresses the crowd.

"How's everybody doing, tonight?"

The responding screams have Vann and me grinning from ear to ear.

"We've got something brand new tonight, something we've never played before. You want to hear it?"

The screaming crowd gets even louder if that's possible, before the lights go down and come back up in a moody, blueish haze. A single spotlight illuminates Ty, center stage.

When the first notes flow from Kess's fingers, my heart nearly stops.

"This one's called 'The Sky At Night'," Ty speaks softly into the mic.

As soon as he starts to sing, I'm flooded by a sob so powerful that I have to wrap my arms around myself to keep from breaking apart into a zillion pieces.

The night before he left. The music in my dream. It was real.

Tears streak my cheeks by the bucketful, and Vann offers me her strength, hooking an arm around my waist and resting her temple against mine. Looking out at the crowd, all that's visible is a sea of phone flashlights, twinkling like so many stars.

We listen to him sing out his grief about his dad, and his regret, and my heart breaks for everything he's lost.

When the next verse begins, Vann squeezes me tighter.

> *"Like the ghosts of my mistakes,*
> *Or an almost forgotten melody,*
> *She haunts me…"*

Stunned, I look at Steady standing on my other side, arms crossed and a proud smile on his weathered face. All he does is point at me and nod.

Every experience I've ever had, everything that's ever happened to me, I had to go through to get here. Without all of it, this incredible moment never would have happened. Vann, Mari, Kess, Ty—the privilege of knowing them and being able to love all the pieces of myself, makes all of the darkness worth it.

I know now he didn't forget about me, and that I hold a piece of his heart, just as he holds a piece of mine. There's no chance of me curbing my tears now, so I let them flow and get lost in the words the beautiful man on stage is singing about me.

About *us*.

At the end of the song, the lights go dark and the band leaves the stage, while the crowd goes absolutely crazy.

Kess sees us first, and the look on his face immediately tells me who helped plan this. He strides over and picks Vann up, swinging her around once in greeting. His gorgeous smile lights up his entire face.

"You made it."

"Of course we did. I have incredible powers of persuasion when necessary. And if those don't work, I just pout." She laughs as her own smile gets a little brighter.

"Get the fuck out of the way, you oaf. There's time for you to pick up chicks later."

Ty shoves past Kess, pulling off his shirt and wiping his face with it. He claps his best friend on the back and turns to see who he's talking to.

The instant he registers it's me standing in front of him, all waterlogged and emotional, his own eyes fill with tears.

"Hali."

"Hi, Ty."

He takes three strides toward me and crushes his lips to mine, wrapping one hand in my hair and pulling me tightly against his body with the other.

Our friends start cheering and clapping, and soon everybody else at the side of the stage joins in, even though they have no idea what they're celebrating.

He breaks our kiss and searches my face like he's trying to memorize it.

"What's wrong?"

"Absolutely nothing," he answers with certainty.

He smoothes my hair behind my ears and rests his forehead against mine.

"I don't know what we take with us when our time here is up, but just in case, when we're old and gray and my time has come, I want the memory of this perfect moment to be with me in the next life."

"I won't run from you again, Ty. You're stuck with me now." I give him a teary grin.

"That's good because I'm not letting you go."

Hali

The white sheets are cool against my tanned skin and rustle softly as I stretch.

"Good morning, Beautiful," my favorite silken voice purrs next to my ear.

I smile and open my eyes to see him in bed beside me, propped up on one elbow.

"Mmmmmmm," I murmur, stretching again, enjoying the feel of the soft cotton against my back.

"You need to stop doing that."

"Stop doing what?"

"Every time you stretch, your tits press against the sheet and push it a little lower."

Looking down at myself, I see that I'm barely covered up to my nipples. I also take note of something else.

"Where exactly is your hand?" I arch an eyebrow and smirk.

He just smiles wickedly at me and maintains eye contact.

Holding the material against my chest with one hand, I use the other to pull it off of him and he doesn't even flinch.

"Oh sure, complain about my tits while you're jerking off right beside me." I swallow thickly, the slow, rhythmic movement as he strokes himself a huge turn-on.

"It wasn't a complaint."

"No? What was it then?"

"A warning."

In one smooth motion, he rips the sheet away from me and slips between my naked thighs. He braces himself with a tattooed forearm on either side of my head and slowly slides his rock-hard cock deep into me. He pauses for a beat and locks his gaze with mine. He gives me a small, private smile and starts moving, rolling his hips against me.

When his teeth nip gently up the side of my neck, I moan quietly, and he knows this is going to be a quickie. He reaches his hand down between us and starts rubbing my clit.

"Come with me," he whispers and caresses my ear lobe with the tip of his tongue.

The wave of pleasure builds until I can't stand it

anymore, and just as I peak, I feel him throb within me as he finds his own release.

"Now that is a fantastic way to wake up." He drops a soft kiss on my lips. Standing, he stretches his hands toward the ceiling and then out to the side before padding to the bathroom completely naked.

I hear the shower turn on, and pull the sheet back over me, curling up on my side with a satisfied grin.

It's been fifteen months since that night backstage in London. Fifteen months that have changed my entire existence.

I haven't been back to Folkestone since I left for The Overlook. Instead, when Ty asked, and Kess had no issue with it, I made the decision to move into the house they share in the Hollywood Hills.

They threw me an incredible party for my nineteenth birthday, and my mother gave me the best gift she ever could—my freedom. I haven't seen her since she dropped me off in Puget Sound, and only spoken to her a handful of times, but the day I turned nineteen, a courier showed up at our door with a registered letter. She had made arrangements with the firm handling the money my father left me to release my trust, rather than waiting until twenty-one. An appointment at their offices in San Francisco and seven signatures later, I was independently wealthy.

When the guys found out the dollar amount, they both choked on their dinner. At least Ty knows I'm not with him for his money. Now he likes to tell people it's his body that I'm all about, which Kess and Vann find hilarious.

These days, Vann spends more time here than in Michigan. Neither one of them has said a word, and we don't have any actual evidence, but both Ty and I think there might be something going on between her and Kess. The band just released its third album, and The Sky At Night is the first single. They'll be gearing up for another tour soon, and whether I stay or go with them, I'd love to be able to have Vann around.

"Hey, Hals," Ty calls, poking his head out of the shower. "There's this spot on my back that I can't seem to reach. How about you come and give a guy a hand?"

I grin and roll off the bed, more than happy to join him.

"Good morning, Kess." I pat him on the head as I pass him on my way to the coffeemaker.

Just as I hit start on the fancy machine, the buzzer for the front gate sounds.

"Expecting anybody?" he asks, moving to check the security monitor attached to the wall in the pantry.

"Nope. Who is it?"

"Looks like a delivery guy." He pushes the intercom button. "What do you need, dude?"

We both watch the kid on the monitor as he gets spooked at Kess's voice seemingly coming out of nowhere.

"Uh, I have a delivery for a Harriet T-t-torsten?" He stutters and waves an envelope.

Kess can't contain his laughter while he pushes the button to open the gate. He's known for a while what my birth name is, but every time he hears it, he finds it extra entertaining.

I flick his ear as I leave the kitchen and it only makes him laugh harder.

The kid is getting out of his delivery van as I open the front door.

"I'm Hali Torsten. You have something for me?"

He looks like he's about to say something when his face suddenly goes pasty white and his mouth clamps shut. Practically throwing the thick envelope at me, he dashes back into his vehicle and peels down the driveway.

"You really need to stop scaring the delivery boys. We're starting to get a reputation up here." I turn around and give Ty a quick kiss on the cheek before pinching his ass.

Back in the kitchen, I drop into the chair across from Kess, and Ty sets a coffee mug down in front of me. I slip my finger under the flap on the fancy envelope bearing my sister's return address and rip it open.

"It looks like an invitation." That might be a

commonplace occurrence to most people, but for me, it's still somewhat of a rarity unless it comes through one of the guys or Vann. Pulling the embossed card out, I read it with my heart in my throat. Then I read it a second time just to be sure.

"What does it say, Hals?" Ty asks.

"Yeah, you're killing us here," Kess laments.

"I guess it's time to go back to Folkestone." I swallow a mouthful of coffee, hoping it extinguishes the flare of anxiety in my gut.

"How do you guys feel about weddings?"

Want to know more about Hali's past? Start the Folkestone Sins series with Fragile Things today!

Will Kess and Vann each find their happiness? And who the heck is getting married back in Folkestone? Find out in The Sea At Dawn.

Stay up to date on all release news and goodies! Like my Facebook page, join my reader group, and sign up for my newsletter today.

ALSO BY SAMANTHA LOVELOCK

Folkestone Sins

Now Available

Fragile Things (Folkestone Sins Book 1)

Fractured Things (Folkestone Sins Book 2)

Restless Things (Folkestone Sins Book 3)

Ruined Things (Folkestone Sins Book 4)

Coming Soon

Wounded Things (Folkestone Sins Book 5)

Heroin Heartbreak

Now Available

The Sky At Night (Heroin Heartbreak Book 1)

Coming 2025

The Sea At Dawn (Heroin Heartbreak Book 2)

PLAYLIST

Hali

Available on Spotify

'Alive' - Zeds Dead, MKLA

'No God In Thunderdome' - HEALTH

'Glass House' - Machine Gun Kelly, Naomi Wild

'Broken' - Palaye Royale

'All Comes Crashing' - Metric

'Casualty' - MOTHICA

'after dark x sweater weather' - slo, twilight, Tazy

'Save Me' - Jelly Roll

'BITCH' - GG Magree, Royal & the Serpent

'The Madness' - Foreign Air

'Haunt Me' - Kaskade, The Moth & The Flame

'Jealousy' - Jacob Lee

'Keeping Me Alive' - Jonathan Roy

'Wicked Game' - Lusaint

'madhouse' - Nessa Barrett

'Panic Room' - Au/Ra

'Walk with Fire' - Hunter As a Horse

'Too Long' - RIBS

'What You're Missing' - TENDER

'Haunted' - Isabel LaRosa

'Fire Escape' - Call Me Karizma

'Fool' - So Below, Tom Young

'Get Out' - YONAKA

'Dichotomy (Intro)' - GG Magree

'Stream of Consciousness' - Solv

'Hot Blooded' - New Constellations

'Come To Me' - Johnny Goth

'Witch Hunt' - Chandler Leighton, DEZI

'Never Land - A Fragment' - Sisters of Mercy

'Good Ones' - Charli XCX

'Acid Rain' - Lorn

Available on Spotify

'blood' - nothing,nowhere ft. KennyHoopla & Judge
'Without Me' - Fame on Fire
'Hills Have Eyes' - POORSTACY
'Bottle and Mary Jane' - Jelly Roll
'No Love in LA' - Palaye Royale
'Masterpiece' - Motionless in White
'Faithless' - The Airborne Toxic Event
'Destructible' - Siiickbrain
'Arizona' - Highly Suspect
'insubordinate' - alt.

'Bleach' - Hurtwave

'Suffocate' - Cold

'Simple Man' - Deftones

'In Our Blood' - Redlight King

'Blackout' - Manafest, Sam Tinnesz

'Dead Man Walking' - Jelly Roll

'Take Me Away' - Ayron Jones

'You Know Me Too Well' - Nothing But Thieves

'Rockstar' - Blue Stahli

'Demons' - Jacob Lee

'Dream On' - Blacktop Mojo

'Scars' - Boy Epic

'Ocean' - Kody West

'Heavy Heart' -Redlight King

'Disinjectant' - Matt Lange

'Passenger' - Boston Manor

'Eye of a Hurricane' - Redlight King

ACKNOWLEDGMENTS

Writing this book was one of the hardest things I've ever done. Since my father passed away in December of 2021, life has been very different for me. So many things were left unresolved, and I'm learning how to deal with that.

I am so eternally grateful to all of the readers who stuck around, the new readers who gave this book a chance, and everybody who believed in and supported me.

To my team, the Cliffbanger Queens, your continuous and unwavering support is something I don't even know how to thank you for. I love you all.

Lee, you help make things bearable. Thank you for your friendship. Sorry, you're stuck with me forever now.

Sarah and Melly, I know I'm a pain in the ass to both of you in different ways. Thank you for being two people in the book world I can always talk to.

All of the amazing authors and bookish support people I've had the pleasure to meet and work with, thank you for your kindness, your grace, and your friendship.

Boo Radley, thank you for putting up with my shit. I know it hasn't been easy and I love you for smiling through it all. Winnie and I wouldn't know what to do without you.

Mum, thank you for finally coming to your senses and moving here. The dinners, cookies, and conversations are something that I missed.

To all of my friends and family, thank you again for your support, your love, and your tolerance of my being forgetful and absent.

ABOUT THE AUTHOR

Samantha Lovelock is a USA Today Bestselling author of captivating contemporary new adult romance novels. Known for her clever wordplay and love for cliffhangers, her stories are filled with emotion, passion, and intrigue, leaving readers on the edge of their seats.

When she's not engrossed in her writing, Samantha enjoys indulging in graphic design, good books, scary movies, and the decadence of dark chocolate.

Samantha resides in the stunning Canadian Rockies with her British cowboy and their furbaby, Winston Churchill.

www.samanthalovelock.com

facebook.com/samanthalovelockwrites

instagram.com/authorsamanthalovelock

tiktok.com/@samanthalovelock

amazon.com/~/e/B089RS6578

goodreads.com/samanthalovelock

bookbub.com/profile/samantha-lovelock

THE SKY AT Night

USA TODAY BESTSELLING AUTHOR

SAMANTHA LOVELOCK